CUTHBERT
Death's Valley

#4

by

Patrick Barrett

A Wild Wolf Publication

Published by Wild Wolf Publishing in 2016
Copyright © 2016 Patrick Barrett

ISBN: 978-1-907954-53-5
Also available as an e-book

www.wildwolfpublishing.com

Chapter 1

Percy and Cuthbert lay on their backs cloud-watching. From the top of the hill they stared up at the mashed potato formations slowly morphing into each other. The sunlight flickered momentarily as a bird passed overhead.

Cuthbert smiled as Percy grumbled and pulled out the oily rag from a secret recess in his jacket. Rolling onto his side he watched Percy rubbing away at his shoulder.

"Supposed to be good luck you know, Percy." He felt a warm splash on his neck.

Percy stopped rubbing. "Have you noticed how we seem to get more good luck than most?" he asked. "Where's that flaming crow?"

The Valley had settled into a warm lazy summer. Percy still wore his tweed jacket and his trademark 'Turned down wellies'; his only concession to the climate was a knotted handkerchief to keep the sun off his head. Whilst Percy swore by its effectiveness, Cuthbert thought it looked ridiculous on top of his cap and the furse-bush of red hair. Cuthbert had left his jacket off, rolled up his sleeves and displayed his braces. In this rural farming community he was almost ready to feature in a scandalous magazine!

The two resumed their afternoon's obsession.

Cuthbert could see cloud-giant mythical figures striding across the sky - blending seamlessly into white horses crashing through the surf - trailing away like lost thoughts on the breeze.

Percy saw potatoes!

Always potatoes: mashed potatoes, boiled potatoes, or bags of potatoes! It took Cuthbert ages to get Percy to study the clouds and recognise it as a pastime. One special afternoon Percy had his eureka moment. He saw potatoes! But Cuthbert was protected against Percy.

Whereas his friend had holes in his imagination, Cuthbert had holes in his perception. This meant that he could blank-out whole sections of Percy and still stay sane. Of course, this is probably the only example ever of 'Cuthbert' and 'sane' appearing in the same sentence. Percy seemed more relaxed these days. He managed his garden beautifully, although Cuthbert didn't exactly know where it was. He also started to help around the farm, but Cuthbert hadn't seen

3

any evidence of it. In fact, a swan left more of a ripple passing through water than Percy left passing through life.

"Any plans for today?" asked Cuthbert mischievously.

Percy was staring contentedly at a magnificent pile of King Edwards passing overhead, chewing on a grass stalk. "Oh, just the usual," he said dreamily.

"I thought we could perhaps go somewhere for a change," said Cuthbert.

Neither of them left the valley if they could avoid it, but it was nice to see Percy panic. In the heat of the afternoon Percy just mumbled, "Can't think of anywhere better than this."

Cuthbert recognised the sleepy tone and rolled onto his front. Percy could not be provoked. To all intents and purposes Percy was asleep!

Cuthbert scanned the top of the hill and spotted a hunched figure sitting alone. Instead of shouting or waving, Cuthbert began to walk towards the figure.

'Whistle' had not made the slightest concession to the heat. His hood was pulled up over his head and he stared intently down into the empty reservoir. Cuthbert assumed the hood was to blur the image seen by the fish and fool them onto Whistle's hook.

But the fact was that no-one knew what Whistle looked like. If you didn't talk into the front of the hood he couldn't hear you, and his own voice was muffled unless he faced you. Cuthbert knew his name was Entwhistle, and that the family had been valley-bound forever. Apparently, this had been the family's fishing spot for generations and when the reservoir was built they claimed squatters rights. The fact that there were no fish in it didn't deter them either!

Whenever Cuthbert voiced the theory that *You won't catch anything in there mate*, the reply was always the same. *Whistle see, Cuthbert, Whistle see.*

Approaching the hunched figure Cuthbert came on a startling idea. If he didn't know who 'Whistle' was, he could be any one of them! It could even be him.

Steady on Cuthbert, he thought. *This is the sort of thing which ends with you arguing with your own reflection!* In fact he had done that very thing this morning, until Percy had looked at him strangely.

4

Pulling himself together and blaming the lack of oxygen and the heat, Cuthbert spoke towards the front of the hood, "Afternoon, Whistle, caught anything yet?"

The hood jerked slightly. "Oh Cuthbert, Whistle be the death of each other we shall. You startled me."

Cuthbert sat down beside him and dangled his feet over the dry chamber below. "That's a cheerful thought for a sunny day Whistle, feeling down are we?"

Some people used silence to punctuate their speech. Whistle used it to punctuate it before he spoke. Eventually he asked, "Been busy lately, Cuthbert?"

Not really concentrating, Cuthbert said, "Oh, you know what it's like running a farm, always something to do."

The hood nodded sagely. "Not much in the way of undertaking then?"

Cuthbert laughed, "You know, I'd forgotten about that Whistle. No, it's been very quiet."

The hood turned slowly towards Cuthbert. "A man has deep thoughts battling with the forces of nature day in and day out, you know Cuthbert."

Cuthbert nodded politely until he realised that Whistle meant fishing in an empty hole! "Do you think it might be time for a holiday, Whistle?"

After a silence, Cuthbert heard, "Whistle sleep long enough after we're gone, or do you think Whistle live forever in the valley Cuthbert?"

Finding himself deep in thought, which was strange territory indeed, Cuthbert didn't notice Whistle leave. Or at any rate, he was gone when Cuthbert looked around. Somehow, Whistle had touched upon something.

Running back down the hill, Cuthbert grabbed Percy by the lapels and shook him, causing Percy's face to blur and his knotted hankie to fall off.

Cuthbert found himself shrieking, "Nobody's died Percy, nobody's died!"

Percy waited for his brain to stabilise after the shaking, and stammered, "You haven't quite got the hang of panicking, have you Cuthbert? You are supposed to do it when *everybody* is dead."

Percy broke free and moved away, in case Cuthbert started shaking him again. It wasn't too bad when he was asleep, but who knew what might happen when his thoughts were running around in there?

Cuthbert sat wide-eyed, "When is the last time anybody died in the Valley?"

Percy replaced his knotted hankie. "It was very close about three seconds ago, mate!" He was studying his friend closely.

Cuthbert burble about 'Checking his records'.

That should be a laugh! thought Percy. Standing, he followed Cuthbert down the hill.

Chapter 2

The Captain and Henry were strolling together. Whilst the Valley was undeniably peaceful these two had seen some of the World, and echoes of real life sometimes surfaced.

"I miss the camaraderie of the Forces you know," the Captain was saying.

Henry nodded. He had been a war reporter and television presenter, without getting too involved with either. "It had some moments I suppose."

The Captain continued, "That brother of yours, Ronald, has he really been everywhere he claims to have been?"

Henry laughed, "He doesn't carry a passport, he carries an atlas! Every conflict from Afghanistan to Zaire carries Ronald's thumbprint, or the thumbprint of whomever he was pretending to be that week anyway! Wherever I was sent somehow he was always there before me. To tell the truth, most of my scoops came from Ronald. Usually he either found the body, seen the body, or caused the body!"

The Captain nodded, "Cuthbert's heading this way at a good lick, think something is wrong?"

Henry squinted up the hill. "Percy doesn't seem unduly panicked, does he?"

The Captain shaded his eyes, "How would we tell?"

Henry composed his face and prepared to show interest, but Cuthbert went steaming past them without a word.

"Well!" huffed the Captain. "It would have been nice if we ignored him before he ignored us!"

Henry turned his attention to Percy, who was sauntering towards them. "Anything wrong?" he asked, seeing the expression on the little chap's face. "Can you speak?"

Percy resembled a distressed bovine. His mouth was trying to scribe a circle around his nose and his eyes were locked in the middle.

"Has Cuthbert gone for an ambulance?" asked the Captain.

Percy made a huge effort, swallowed, and all his features returned to where they should be. "That's better," he spluttered. "Swallowed my piece of grass and it was trying to get back out my nose!" Adopting a formal tone, he continued, "Gentlemen, if you would care to follow me, I believe there is entertainment afoot."

Striding smartly he set off after Cuthbert, and the two friends exchanged curious glances and followed on.

Chapter 3

"You keep your records in a coffin?" spluttered the Captain.

Cuthbert paused from flicking through his files, "Why not There's no point it just being a big empty space, is there? And anyway, they are records of deaths and burials after all!"

Henry looked over Cuthbert's shoulder, and asked, "Is that all of them?"

Cuthbert dropped a file back into its slot and stretched his back, "No, those two are full as well. They cover all my father's internments too."

Henry strode over to the other two coffins laid horizontally on trestles. Percy was sitting on top of one, and he jumped off reluctantly when Henry waved him away.

Henry gripped the edges of the lid, and turning to Cuthbert asked, "Are they alphabetical, will these be the A's?"

Cuthbert looked at Henry in surprise, "No, of course not. Mr. and Mrs. Hayes will be under H. Good job I am the undertaker around here, we wouldn't know where the bodies were!"

Henry bit back a retort. Glancing into the coffin, he said, "Well, we certainly know where this one is!"

The room became silent even by the standards of a mortuary. Morbid curiosity threw a noose around them and they were all pulled inwards to stare at a beautifully embalmed corpse.

Percy cackled with glee. "I told you! I could feel it in my bones!"

Cuthbert glared at him. With a large screwdriver in his hand, he hissed, "Shut up Percy, or you'll feel this in your bones as well!" Then scratching his head, added, "I wonder where I buried the records?"

Chapter 4

A man should always have ambition. Marvin Middlewick had always been ambitious.

When he had first joined the Local Authority he sensed he was destined for greatness. All those doors with names on them, all those corridors leading to an established hierarchy, it was pointless being ambitious when you didn't know who to suck up to next!

At the moment he was worried he'd been promoted sideways. The obvious way to advance was by way of *dead men's shoes.* As the old and the bold died out, the young and dynamic were supposed to take over. The trouble was, Martin had taken so long moving up that he was now one of the 'old and bold', and those above simply refused to die out!

He lovingly handled his new desk plaque. He told everyone it was a present from an admirer. Tongues had wagged in the corridors for weeks, until he included the cost on his expenses form and rather gave the game away. He ran his finger over the raised letters, admiring the gold leaf. 'Marvin Middlewick – C.L.O.S.E.D,' it read.

The plaque initially faced his door to greet visitors but resulted in people entering, glancing at the plaque, muttering 'Oh sorry' and leaving again. Eventually Marvin turned it round to face him - that way he could appreciate the full scope of his new title and job description.

Marvin Middlewick - **C**ouncil **L**iaison **O**fficer **S**upervising **E**xcavations and **D**igging. He had come a long way! Those jealous barbs of 'Oh, work for the Council do you?' were neatly avoided by simply not mixing with that sort!

The file was laid equidistant on his desk and he was taunting himself with it. All through the Times crossword, and the obituaries, he ignored it to allow the tension to mount.

One of the obituaries caught his eye. A mercenary named Ronald Mandrake was being remembered. The man had virtually saved the world single-handed! Why did we only hear about interesting people when they no longer here? *Huh!* thought Marvin, *He wouldn't have lasted two minutes with these pressures.*

He opened the folder and began to read. His speed reading abilities came to the fore and only the relevant words registered. Valley - registration of burials - no forms received - fly tipping?

Marvin formed a steeple with his fingers. "Negligent form filling, negligent payment of fees and negligent disposal of remains," he muttered. Suddenly, he realised why this office needed a man of his calibre.

Cuthbert now had two bodies and one coffin full of files. The files covered most of his father's work. The bodies were definitely Cuthbert's handiwork.

Percy gripped the edge of one of the coffins and pulled himself up on tip-toes. Peering in, he said, "I thought no-one died lately?"

Cuthbert scratched his head, "They haven't, these two were some of my first. It was hectic back then. Nobody believed that I was the new undertaker and by the time they *had* to believe it, there was a backlog."

Henry was flicking through a file, and asked, "Aren't there laws covering losing bodies, Cuthbert?"

Cuthbert paled. If there was one instruction he remembered from his father, it was: "Cuthbert, try not to lose *another* body!"

Percy came to the rescue. "He hasn't actually lost them though, has he?" he said nodding to the two coffins. "They're still in God's waiting room."

The Captain snorted, "Remind me to take a ticket when I pop-off, then I will know when my number's up. Hah! Number's up, I like that!" Chuckling away to himself the Captain took his leave and set off home.

Henry placed the file back in its place, asking, "So, how many plots have you got spare Cuthbert?"

Cuthbert studied Henry's face as if he would find the answer there. "Plots?" he asked vacantly.

Henry peered suspiciously at him. "You do have a cemetery map all marked out with numbered plots don't you?" Henry looked at Percy and was rewarded with a shrug, so pressed on, "So how do you know where to bury anyone?"

Cuthbert brightened, "Oh, that's easy, a grave always leaves a hump, so I just go between them."

A sudden suspicion assailed Henry, "Cuthbert, it is hallowed ground isn't it?"

An indignant Cuthbert retorted, "Of course it is. I hollow it out with a spade or there wouldn't be a hole."

Henry was really struggling now, "Hallowed, not hollowed! Cuthbert, is there a priest present when you bury someone?"

Percy grinned, chiming in, "Only if he's the one being buried!"

Henry was appalled. "What about pall-bearers?"

Cuthbert was astounded, "Too expensive."

Percy added, "He borrows my wheelbarrow."

Henry sat down heavily, "So you don't know where anyone is?"

Cuthbert was affronted, "Of course I do. They are all over there." He gave a vague wave which took in most of the hillside.

Percy gave Henry a playful thump on the shoulder, saying, "Cheer up mate. Who on earth is going to check?"

Chapter 5

Marvin Middlewick stared into his full length mirror; his was the only office to have a mirror and a coat stand. Most of the younger employees loved the coat stand until they discovered that it wasn't for throwing hoops at. Marvin checked his appearance and nodded to his reflection with approval. Serious business warranted a serious demeanour, and Marvin looked seriously serious.

Feeling like the last bastion of honest society against the creeping tide of corruption, he recalled his father's wisdom. *"Marvin, always remember son, whilst opportunity knocks, temptation leans on the doorbell!"*

With those wise words his father had left home with the Swedish Au-Pair wearing Bermuda shorts and a huge smile!

As Marvin knew, the wisest words came from the most experienced culprits. Closing the door behind him, Marvin surveyed the main operations room, not for him, the hen-coop partitions and background babble of the lesser minions.

Straightening his shoulders into a posture of ramrod authority he strode purposefully out into the real world.

Chapter 6

The kitchen table groaned quietly as Cuthbert, Percy and Henry, settled around it with mugs of coffee.

People thought it was the age of the timber causing these sounds, but it was actually ritual abuse. You start out in life as a noble tree bending before the wind just so that it doesn't get a complex, and you end up sitting here having your top thumped and stretchers kicked. It was older than anyone in the room and a king once hid in its branches. No wonder its joints ached!

The three friends around the table were starting to suspect that the peaceful summer was coming to an end and the knocking at the door seemed to confirm it.

Cuthbert immediately had visions of every past visitor he ever had; none of those events had ended well.

Percy was inundated with thoughts of past misunderstandings, which may even now be outside and trembling with anticipation of a reunion.

Henry simply heard a knock at the door. What possible harm could come from sitting with two companions drinking coffee? Looking at his friends he suddenly knew exactly what could go wrong - *everything!*

Being awkward, like everything else in the house, the door simply refused to answer itself. After all, it had people to do that surely?

Henry opened the door, assuming he was greeting one of Cuthbert's colleagues.

The man wore a sombre suit and a sombre expression. Entering the kitchen he gave a small bow to the occupants before setting his briefcase on the table.

"Would you care for a coffee?" asked Henry politely, trying to make up for the waxworks tableaux at the table.

This man reeked of officialdom and Cuthbert and Percy had gone into 'rabbit in the headlights' mode.

The man seemed about to accept, until he glanced into Percy's cup and spotted a steaming blue sludge. Percy had a nasty habit of stirring his tea with a biro and leaving it in until all the ink leaked out. He had once been approached by an agent and offered party bookings. What with the red hair, cap and turned down wellies, the blue lips just seemed to be part of his act.

Declining the offer, Marvin sat down and opened his briefcase.

The file slid out into his hand, terrorising the room in the way that plain-covered files do the world over. Marvin tried to never show a lack of knowledge to a lesser order, and so he did a visual check on the fingernails of the two men seated before him so as to identify the errant undertaker. Marvin noted the soil on one of them and addressed Percy. "Our new computer system has revealed that you have not sent in the requisite forms for several years."

"Haven't I?" asked Percy, wondering how this twerp had found him. "Did you send me any?"

Marvin looked momentarily annoyed. "Of course we did. We are the Local Authority, that is what we do."

Marvin perched a pair of half-moon spectacles on the bridge of his nose and peered at Percy. "Can you supply me with details of where everything is buried?" he asked. His voice had the quality of a rat-trap made of silk.

Percy scratched his head, "Well," he began." I usually put the same types in the same place whenever I can so they won't be hard to find, plus the soil is softer from regular use."

Marvin asked, "Same types?" He was impressed. "Do you have an inter-denominational plot?" he asked thirsting for details.

Noting that this seemed to impress the official, Percy ran with it. "Oh yes, I always inter-dominate, if you don't space them out they end up all tangled up!"

Marvin was scribbling furiously with an old-fashioned fountain pen, "And how many different sections do you have?"

Percy pretended to count mentally on his fingers and came up with 'fourteen'. He then had a memory flash, adding, "Sorry, fifteen. I always forget the Swedes."

Marvin was more impressed than he had ever been. He laid down his pen and said, "You have taken the trouble to create an international plot as well? This is wonderful. Our diversity department can use this for filling our quota for this year."

He closed his briefcase, stood, shook Percy's hand vigourously, and said, "Thank you, pleasure to meet you. I can't wait to audit your forms and pay a proper visit to the graveyard. Goodbye."

Percy took a sip of his coffee and said through blue lips, "What a nice man, obviously misses his Mum."

Henry walked home, alone with his thoughts. Whenever he spent time with Cuthbert and Percy he was always left feeling the same. It all seemed quite normal on the face of it, but there was the suspicion that it would spiral out of control very quickly and very soon. He wondered how long it would take the pair of them to decide that Percy's vegetable plot hadn't been the subject of the discussion.

"You clot!" ranted Cuthbert. "He will come back and expect to find Arlington National Cemetery half-way up the hill."

Percy looked puzzled. "Why would he do that?"

Cuthbert sat heavily, explaining, "Because you told him there was a plot split into different religions and nationalities."

"Isn't there?" asked Percy.

Chapter 7

Marvin was puzzled. He had been laughed at! Marvin did not like being laughed at. He was an official of the Local Authority. In a communist country he would have his own Trabant saloon!

He didn't like being puzzled either, unless it was Sunday morning and the culprit was the crossword! That was fine. The compiler was paid to try to outwit him personally on a weekly basis, but this was unprecedented.

It was a real surprise. She had seemed such a nice lady. After entering the museum he showed his card to the curator.

Geraldine read the card aloud, 'Marvin Middlewick - C.L.O.S.E.D.' She smirked and asked if he was '*Open* to suggestions!' She seemed to find this highly amusing.

Marvin introduced himself in his role as the **C**ouncil **L**iaison **O**fficer **S**upervising **E**xcavations and **D**igging, and began with a gentle reminder that he must be informed of forthcoming digs carried out by the museum. All had gone well enough, until he mentioned how impressed he was with the local undertaker and his organisational skills.

Geraldine stared, she had tried mind distraction techniques and she even pictured Marvin in his underwear. But in the end she gave up and collapsed across her desk howling with laughter, thumping it from time to time as the pain gave some relief.

Now, Marvin wasn't a complete stranger to women, he had almost proposed marriage but the lady in question was unavailable on the day he allocated for the proposal. She was now Chief Executive Officer to some giant corporation, but that was her loss!

Of course, Marvin was now ecstatically entrenched with his beloved '*Doreeen!*' His fingers clenched and his eyes automatically became slits as he acknowledged her name.

Marvin stared at the woman before him, giggling helplessly. He was left with the feeling that he was 'out of the loop' or something. He chided himself for this modern expression. He tried to ignore it because he had no idea where the loop, was or why he should want to be in it. The problem was, the more he ignored it, the more his brain demanded an explanation.

Back at the office he laid the file carefully on his desk and then opened his door slightly. Was it his imagination or did several people exchange glances when he came back in? His 'In tray' was still empty. He had not been sent any new assignments. He made sure that the door handle functioned okay and returned to his desk.

A sudden burst of laughter from outside made him hesitate, before beginning his day's report. He didn't socialise with anyone from the office, perhaps he was missing something.

Wandering across to the water cooler he spotted two office juniors heatedly discussing who was going for the extra stationery allocation. It was a hated task because of all the form filling, meant that whoever fetched it would be late home.

Marvin appeared behind the two girls, just as one of them said, "Well, *someone's got to go!*" Then they spotted the Head of Department, giggled self-consciously and walked away.

Marvin was appalled, not another 'cost-cutting' session! He remembered the last time; all his contemporaries suddenly became passionate about gardening and disappeared.

The office resembled a kindergarten overnight as it had been filled with young people sitting at their desks with wires coming out of their ears and 'jigging away' to their own heartbeats. Every computer screen was topped off by some kind of small stuffed creature and it became a habit to raise one's hand only to have someone else slap it!

Safely back in his office, Marvin pondered. The only way up for his age group was promotion. The only way for promotion was after a death. *Dead men's shoes,* he thought, *dead men's shoes*.

Chapter 8

Back at El Rancho Cuthbert, Percy still couldn't see the problem.

"Good grief, Cuthbert," he said, "You have seen other cemeteries. Tidy yours up, paint some bits white, put a flag up and Bob's your Uncle!"

Cuthbert stopped pacing, "Do you think he would help?"

"Who do you mean?" Percy asked.

Cuthbert sighed impatiently, "My uncle Bob."

Percy was struck by a strange thought. "Cuthbert, you have *seen* another cemetery, haven't you?"

The gates to the Heavenly Way Internment Complex were an elaborate affair with stone angels blowing trumpets on top of the gate-posts.

"Looks like they've got their own band," said Percy.

A second sign just inside the gates stated:

We are the first step on the stairway to heaven.

Cuthbert and Percy marched up the ruler-straight gravel driveway into a discreet crematorium where piped heavenly music soothed the senses. Chairs were laid in straight lines and velvet curtains covered the end wall. A huge mural was on the other wall where even more angels blew trumpets, clouds billowed, and a bearded man consulted a ledger.

"Huh!" said Cuthbert huffily, "That's not very professional. At least I pay attention when people come to me. If I had time to read books I wouldn't bury many!"

Percy spoke at his shoulder, "Actually, you don't bury many at all!"

Cuthbert sensed Percy wandering off and he let the music calm his soul. The moment of contemplation was shattered by a shout.

"Hey Cuthbert, this is poor security." Percy had pulled the velvet drapes apart and opened a heavy circular door, "He's left his safe open!"

The man had been expecting them, but he hadn't been expecting *them*! At first he wondered who left the gates open until he realised that these two were the 'clients' who had offered payment in return for his expertise. Apparently they were seeking to emulate his dauntingly high standards.

As he showed them around his crematorium, Percy asked nervously, "Is that the smell of death?"

The owner sniffed and replied, "No, that's Gerald, he puts a meat pie on top of the oven ready for his lunch."

Outside they were shown the smart little digger, bright yellow and equipped with a bucket just the right size to scoop out the perfect grave.

"No shovels here mate," whispered Percy nudging Cuthbert.

The office had a wall covered in filing cabinets and a huge map showing every plot, numbered and colour-coded.

"Is that so they can find their way back?" asked Percy.

The owner was not amused. "When the departed find rest with us, they stay at rest!"

Outside, very close to the gates, the tour came to an end. Percy pumped the man's hand and thanked him profusely as Cuthbert edged even closer to the gate.

"Ahem" coughed the owner, "There was talk about payment for the advice." He looked expectantly at Percy.

Percy cocked his head to one side, "Oh we knew all about that mate, we just wanted to see which bits were painted white and what flag we needed, bye!" And with that, he skipped out of the gate and joined Cuthbert beyond them.

The owner watched them go gritting his teeth. He was picturing the pair of them laid out, hands folded across their chests, and ready to go into a bin-bag. He could hear the music. Oh, *the music*.

Turning around he faced the long walk back up the drive. The cheek of it, how could they possibly hope to emulate anything he had created here, and where the devil had his flag gone?

Chapter 9

After coming across the Captain and Henry again, Percy and Cuthbert described the visit as they sat around in Cuthbert's kitchen. While Cuthbert described the things they had seen, Percy set about emptying his pockets and his wellies onto the table.

The Captain and Henry watched in fascination as a pile of green ornamental gravel dashed across the wooden tabletop every time Percy emptied something onto it. Percy then unravelled a long piece of material from around his waist and flapped it over the pile. The flag had a design of two interlocking gears on it.

"Isn't that an award for industry?" asked Henry.

Percy looked pleased, "It's come to the right chap then."

Marvin could see the answer to his problem very clearly.

Public Relations Department was the new religion; this inter-denominational cemetery laid out with all due respect for all nationalities was a winner! This would make his name.

He would wear his Local Authority tie to every function and would be the ambassador for his trade! This was his moment, but it must be jealously guarded. He sellotaped the file to the underneath of his desk drawer; this was his pension, his future. He looked at the empty in-tray and wondered where he could buy some hoops to play with his coat-rack!

The Captain looked first at Percy and then at Cuthbert, before asking, "So you need my organisational skills to invent hundreds of false names, allocate them a random religion, give them all a colour-coded plot and draw a large scale map of where they are not buried?"

The two listeners nodded. "Anything else?" asked the Captain sarcastically. "Got any white paint?" asked Percy.

The Captain couldn't resist a challenge and as boredom seemed to be settling over the valley he strode off to look at the site and prepare his campaign.

Henry noticed that Percy seemed rather subdued, so he sat opposite him and asked what was troubling him. No-one *ever* asked Percy what was troubling him, but boredom really was becoming a problem. Percy looked across the table and shuffled to get comfortable.

Cuthbert saw the movement from where he was sticking fly paper over a crack in a window and eased himself into another room.

"The truth is Henry," began Percy, "It was all the talk of funerals and death. It upset me and it brought back terrible memories."

Henry asked sympathetically, "Was it the loss of your father?"

Percy looked slightly surprised, "Oh no, we knew he was going to get lost. We gave him the wrong map."

Henry tried, "Er no, I meant –"

But Percy went ploughing on, "Right shiftless chap he was, out all hours, never spent a penny if he could help it, and wanted us to think that he was doing several jobs at once and playing the markets with his earnings. Dogs and horses more like."

Henry got the picture, "Lost all the family silver eh?"

Percy looked surprised again, "Oh no, he made millions. He was a terror to the bookies; they took out protection money against him! One time they even kidnapped the horse to stop him betting on it!"

Henry's inner journalist came awake, "I think I remember that."

Percy carried on, "Anyway, we got so sick of him making all this money and not spending any of it on his family, that Mum decided to teach him a lesson. She told him that a cleaning woman friend of hers had overheard a meeting in the city about a new way of training horses. Apparently, these horses had been trained to kill rabbits."

"Rabbits?" said Henry.

"Rabbits!" confirmed Percy. "She told him the training was done on a secluded island away from prying eyes. The trick was to release the rabbit so that it ran down the course, looking like an innocent rabbit."

"Just like the dog track?" asked Henry fascinated.

"Just like the dog track," confirmed Percy patiently. "No-one would expect it at a horse track and it would stop my Dad from winning, because he would be backing the ones he fed the blue pills to, that way the bookies would get some of their money back."

"It sounds very elaborate," mused Henry.

Percy tapped his nose, "Ah, but it had to look real you see. They couldn't use a wubber wabbit like at the dog track."

"Wubber wabbit?" queried Henry, feeling slightly dizzy.

"Sorry," said Percy, "My Dad had a speech defect. Anyway, he pleaded with Mum to tell him where the secret location was. In the end she nicked any old map from the library, drew a cross on it and an arrow pointing to an island. The idea was that after he had spent some time alone on an island trying to identify the horses, he would come to his senses and come back."

Percy slurped his tea noisily and seemed to lose interest in the story.

"*What happened?*" asked Henry. "Did he go?"

Percy shuffled again, "Oh yes, he went, but the island Mum thought was in the Thames was actually the Galapagos Islands, and he was gone for years."

"Did he survive?" asked Henry incredulously.

"Oh yes," said Percy, "Made a fortune racing turtles for visiting sailors and came back loaded."

Henry slumped in his chair, "Well what was so upsetting about death?"

Percy became sombre. "Ahh you see, Dad didn't last long after he came back. After all those years with the turtles we couldn't get him to come out of his shell, and he passed away in his sleep." Percy sat reflecting for a moment.

Henry said, "And you were deeply affected then?"

Percy sat up, "I'll say I was. When his will was read out, he stipulated that all his money should be buried with him, and on the day of the funeral Mum put a box in the coffin with him."

Henry was aghast, "I'm sorry Percy, but surely your Mum wasn't stupid enough to bury his money with him?"

Percy looked at Henry, "Well in a way she drew it all out and wrote him a cheque. She said, *If he can cash it, he can have it!*"

Henry breathed a sigh of relief until Percy added, "Then she lost it all on the horses."

Chapter 10

Henry joined the Captain on the hillside. He was just coming out of his daze. He didn't remember leaving Cuthbert's at all.

The Captain paused in his work to look over the top of his theodolite. "Glad you came to join me Henry, does this look like a graveyard to you? It reminds me of the Somme after it was softened up for an attack!"

Henry shook himself. One of these days he really must ask the Captain how old he was.

The Captain continued, "You've been talking to Percy I see, I recognise the signs."

Ronald surveyed the hillside. The Captain also perused the hillside and *he* had a proper theodolite. So there! Ronald was having difficulty with his survey. The patterned scrim scarf over his face was blurring things and making him sweat.

The Ghillie suit stolen from an incompetent sniper was also cumbersome, with all its leaves and clumps of bracken. Percy had rung him and asked for his help to remove obstacles and prepare the ground for a new cemetery. Ronald explained that this might be difficult because he was dead!

After a short pause, Percy asked, "Will that make you late then?" Sweeping his binoculars around Ronald watched his brother Henry chatting to the Captain. Cuthbert was wandering about with scraps of paper, scratching his head and kicking lumps of stone.

Using his leopard crawling technique Ronald approached Cuthbert and slowly stood.

Cuthbert seeing movement before him in the middle of a graveyard may have been forgiven for thinking he was witnessing a resurrection. Instead he addressed the 'bush' and said, "Oh Hi! Ronald, I thought you were dead!"

The 'bush' slumped visibly and dragged its foliage elsewhere.

This time Henry responded. "Nice obituary Ronald, much better than the last one!"

Ronald gave up after nearing the tripod being used by the surveyor, almost losing his head as the Captain casually swiped the 'bush' out of the way with a machete.

Ronald sat on a discarded log, lifting his camouflaged face veil. Cuthbert, Henry and the Captain, took a break and sat near him.

"Sorry about the obituary, chaps. These foreign intelligence bods are getting quite good. It was time to disappear for a bit."

Henry looked at his brother fondly. "Ronald Mandrake?" he asked.

Ronald gave a smug grin. "Me, of course mixed with the name of your pub, clever eh?" He leaned closer to the group, rustling as his grass and bracken tried desperately to blend in with a mouldy old log. "Always stay close to the truth in an interrogation. While they are busy trying to separate lies from the truth, they don't have time to separate anything else from you! Really affects the concentration when they start that." He shuddered.

The shudder ran through the group as imaginations ran wild. Ronald was the first to realise that the shudder was in the ground itself, and it was followed by rapid clanking. "Tanks!" screamed Ronald. "Take cover, they've found me!" He then 'went tactical' and disappeared.

As the others looked around wildly for Ronald, the source of the noise and somewhere to hide all at the same time, Percy's hat appeared bobbing towards them. It seemed to be riding on a cloud of smoke chased by an appalling din!

Percy waved cheerfully to them from his tractor just as a 'bush' appeared in front of him and threw several smoking cylinders at him. Percy was enveloped in green smoke from one side and red smoke from the other. His tractor emerged from the smoke like a fire-breathing dragon and pinned the 'bush' to the floor. Percy jumped down with a cheery, "Hey Ronald, I thought you were dead."

Ronald was dragged out from under Percy's tractor looking like a half-plucked chicken; bits of twigs and greenery had been chewed from him by the tracks. Switching off the tractor Percy joined the assembly, and the scheme was outlined for Ronald.

Percy hadn't been forgiven yet and Ronald was throwing him some very dirty looks indeed. Ronald absorbed what was needed and rose to the occasion.

What was left of his bush rose with him. "Right," he commandingly said. "I have supplies hidden all around the Valley. We have plenty of explosives, so the first thing is to clear those trees." He pointed to a small copse sprouting from the bumpy ground like hair in an old man's ears. Unwinding a two-colour cord from inside his clothing Ronald led the way into the sparse trees. "This is detonating-cord," he announced. "It is filled with explosive and when we do this …" He wrapped it around the tree trunk and lit one end. The cord disappeared with a loud crack and the tree slowly toppled over, neatly cut in half.

The Captain had seen it before, so had Henry; he had seen it demonstrated on a four-poster bed while he was still in it!

Cuthbert was speechless. Percy was … well, Percy simply ran away!

Ronald watched him go and sneered, "It's the killer stare, it works every time!"

Cuthbert looked away from the smoking stump, nodded to the detonating-cord, and said, "Actually, he's been wearing this stuff to hold his trousers up!"

Marvin was spending more time in the outer office. He prowled around like a predator. Conversation stopped as he approached a booth, but no-one made eye contact with him.

There was only one reason for a senior to behave like this. The staff felt the foetid breath of redundancies over their shoulders. The more suspicious he acted, the more suspicious his staff became.

They all watched each other very closely indeed.

Percy fired up his tractor. Black smoke belched up into the blue sky and the vibrations of the working man ran through him.

Throwing a lever forward he clanked into action, raising the digger arm before him like a king scorpion. The digger dug into the ground and scooped out a trench.

The one at the Heavenly View cemetery had just been wide enough to dig out one grave at a time, but Percy had harnessed some real power to this one. Hydraulic fluid pumped through the arterial hoses and the arm flung and the turret spun. *It could have been set to music*, thought Percy from inside his cab, as he conducted the symphony of mayhem.

Percy started at the well-maintained end of the cemetery. *It looks as if someone really tended this part*, he thought.

Henry came up behind Cuthbert, "Any of your family buried here, Cuthbert?"

Cuthbert wiped away a tear, saying sadly, "Not anymore!"

Percy paid no heed to frantic waving or shouting. There was work to be done, and as long as it only involved pulling levers he was your man! Earth flew, grass flew, broken lids spun through the air like Frisbees. Percy was a one-man redeveloper until he disappeared.

They were all watching at the time. One minute he was there, and the next minute he wasn't. A black plume of smoke hung in the air like an exclamation mark, but the tractor and its operator were nowhere to be seen.

Cuthbert and Henry promptly looked accusingly at Ronald, who shrugged his branches and said, "It wasn't me, he hasn't reached the right spot yet!"

They dashed to where Percy was last seen and stood peering down into a crater. Percy stood beside his tractor, scratching his head. He was inside a large square underground room with a tunnel running into it from uphill, and another running away downhill.

"It's another reservoir," said Cuthbert.

"Looks about as much use as the other one," muttered Ronald.

Henry stroked his chin, saying, "You know, this would hold all the bodies while we flattened the site and started again."

The plan was agreed. Any boxes or remains would be stored in here and re-buried in properly numbered plots after the Inspector had left them alone.

Ronald raised a point, "What about 'One twerp and his tractor,' shall we just start filling it in?"

The Captain said, "No need," and stepped away from the hole.

The digger bucket had appeared over the rim of the hole and crunched into the surface near the edge. Next, Percy threw levers and the tractor climbed up the walls until he sitting there grinning at them from their level again. The new plan was explained and Percy set off once more.

Marvin had developed a tactic. He would walk casually across the main office as if he was leaving the building, then he would suddenly swing around to see who was watching over the cubicle tops.

27

Another one was to stop and clean his spectacles, allowing his eyes to roam while he stood still. The theory was fine, but in practice he couldn't see the nearest cubicle until he put them back on! But the most important action he had taken was to begin... *A list*! Lists had been with Marvin since his inception. Amongst the souvenirs of his birth kept by his mother was a list of all the things she needed to do before he ruined her life forever.

Anyone caught sneaking a look at him made it onto Marvin's lists. He had a list for 'Misuse of toilet breaks'. He had one for those who exaggerated their pencil quota to the detriment of others, but these were just tools of his trade.

The Local Authorities Governing Board believed that the bloodstream was simply a way to convey lists to the brain, and they were its representatives on earth! The new list would show all those conspiring to remove him, it would expose the low-level 'watchers', and would eventually lead him to the men at the top whose jealousy he had aroused.

This was all normal to Marvin. What was slightly unusual was the fact that the list was written on his office wall. It started near the ceiling, (with space left for explanatory notes), and was almost down to the skirting board. An empty in-tray would not make Marvin short of things to do!

Chapter 11

Margery watched Henry carefully.

Typical, she thought, *One minute he was under her feet all day and the next he was missing for hours, and tired when he did appear.'*

"Are you seeing somebody?" she asked.

Henry answered wearily from his chair, "My dear, I am seeing more bodies than I ever wanted to," and with that he was asleep.

Cuthbert's kitchen had been turned into a 'war room.'

The Captain stood at one end with a large sheet of paper on an easel and a pointer. With concentration furrowing his brow he slapped the tip against the paper to emphasise each point as he made it. Apparently, there would be a section for 'Valley folk'- a section for people from another valley - another section for people from foreign valleys - and even a section for people from level areas who simply dropped dead whilst visiting steep valleys! Then there were the belief systems. Some people believed in a greater being, whereas others had trouble believing in themselves.

The Captain and Henry were world travellers and would co-ordinate the colour coding, or they would if Henry could stay awake!

Cuthbert was painfully aware that all the Captain's remarks were made towards him. He knew that it was partly his fault that he was completely responsible, in some small way, by association for what had happened, but couldn't the others pay attention as well?

Risking a quick glance around, Cuthbert saw that Henry was fast asleep again with his head and arms resting on the table.

Percy couldn't stop fidgeting, he had spent hours vibrating away on his tractor and now kept sliding towards the edge of his chair.

"That man there, pay attention!" Cuthbert jumped as the Captain snapped at him. Another sheet of paper had appeared, covered in different coloured blocks. Cuthbert sighed, it was going to be a long evening.

Chapter 12

Avril stared at the man sat on the opposite side of her desk. He sat ramrod straight and perched his briefcase on his knee.

She watched for unusual signs: Facial tics, sudden and jerky movements as if being followed. The trouble was if he really was from the Council, sorry(!) Local Authority, different rules would apply.

Her editor had popped his head around her door, obviously enjoying himself immensely. This man was proposing a full spread to reveal the Valley's cemetery to the world. It would be completely unbiased of course, but must contain many references to some chap named Marvin and his sterling contribution to the effort. The man leaned forward slightly for emphasis and said, "Some of the names in this Valley could soon be known around the world."

Avril muttered, "Believe me, some of them are already known around the world." For some time now Avril had thought she could hear laughter in the outer office, with sounds of attempts to stifle it. Now, she was convinced of it.

"What did this undertaker look like?" she asked as innocently as possible.

Marvin was taken aback; they assured him that he had been allocated a senior reporter. This slip of a girl didn't even know her local undertaker.

Gripping his briefcase tightly, through gritted teeth he described the red-headed little chap with a cap who had impressed him so much. "Salt of the earth he is," insisted Marvin, "Still had the soil on his hands from honest labour!"

The woman before him looked as if she was auditioning for a scene in a movie about the plague! Her mouth jammed shut, her face reddened, and she started banging her hand against the top of her desk just like the museum curator had done.

Was it some strange valley affliction affecting women? thought Marvin as he wrapped his dignity around him and left.

Driving back to the office Marvin pondered the strange turns his life had been taking recently.

Once, being part of a giant soulless organisation full of small soulless people had suited him, but now he wasn't so sure. The whole Department seemed to consider them extremely important these days. Everyone he knew either worked for it, or relied on it in some way. Perhaps it was coming into contact with the outside world which was affecting his outlook.

Realising he had entered the valley, Marvin started to make a detour towards Cuthbert's farm. It surprised him how good the roads were in the Valley.

His Department's budget didn't usually go that far, not after the Christmas fund was topped up anyway!

Turning into Cuthbert's farm gate Marvin was greeted by two huge coaches parked at the farmhouse. *Surely the tourists hadn't started arriving already?* Cuthbert would obviously be busy at the moment, so Marvin reluctantly turned around and continued his journey.

Cuthbert stretched his arms above his head, the work was going well. The Captain and Henry were resting in the new burial chamber and Ronald was out here somewhere, but as he was still in hiding he could be any one of a number of bushes!

Percy had gone back to the farm for some oil; something about the smoke not being thick enough or something! So, Cuthbert was having a moment's peace. Even the thought of a moment's peace seemed to trigger a response in Percy and sure enough there he was charging up the hill towards Cuthbert, little legs pumping, hat bouncing and wellies slapping. As Percy approached he veered towards Cuthbert, gasping frantically.

"Penguins Cuthbert, march of the penguins! Trucks full of them, all over the farm, only just escaped with my life."

A nearby bush said, "Do you know why Polar Bears don't eat penguins?"

Cuthbert looked from Percy to the bush, and said, "Er, no why?"

The bush said, "They can't get the wrappers off!"

The bush then fell backwards holding its sides as Ronald gave in to a moment of levity.

Percy glared at the bush, hissing, "I've got insecticide and I'm not afraid to use it!"

Cuthbert stepped between them, reminding Percy, "Come on mate, you know that the vibration has affected your vision. Last night you thought you had seen the police choir and it was the crow sitting on a fence. (It wasn't recorded what the crow thought it had seen).

Percy calmed down. "Maybe you're right. I can't tell which of you three are speaking to me." He sat down heavily.

Cuthbert wandered off towards the point where he could see the farm below, and stopped dead in his tracks! Dropping flat on his face he turned in the long grass and imitated Ronald's leopard crawl. He promptly bumped into a rock! With a throbbing head and nostrils full of grass seed, Cuthbert returned to Percy.

Percy tried to focus on him, asking, "Well, what did I see. Is it as bad as I thought?"

"Worse," spluttered Cuthbert,

"Where's Ronald?" A nearby bush lazily waved a branch and a sleepy voice said, "What now, Cuthbert?"

Cuthbert slithered over to the bush, peered in and terrified a rabbit!

"This one twit!" said Ronald.

Cuthbert simply addressed *all* the nearby foliage. "They've found you, Ronald. Men in black assault suits carrying violin cases. They've come by the bus load."

Percy jumped up and shouted, "Hah! I'll stop him." He hesitated, "If I knew where he was."

Ronald had gone. There was a trail of twigs and leaves heading towards the new hole.

Two heads appeared over the edge and Henry asked, "What's the matter with Ronald? He's just shot into the tunnels like a rat up a drainpipe."

Cuthbert motioned for silence and led them to the vantage point he had used. "Look, in the farmyard."

"Penguins, thousands of them," said Percy, still trying to focus.

"Men carrying machine guns," said Cuthbert. "Looks like an ambush to me."

"Looks like an orchestra to me!" said the Captain. "How about you Henry?"

Henry smiled, "Cuthbert, I think they *are* simply violin cases."

Cuthbert was embarrassed. "I thought it was the Mafia," he grumbled.

"Wasn't us," said a bush.

"Oh Ronald, you're back," said Cuthbert.

"No, he's gone" said another bush.

Cuthbert looked around in panic. "Are any of these bushes real?"

"Not many, except for the one that clown blew up," said a voice as Jasper led the Valley Mafia home for their tea.

Percy's vision started to clear by the time they had travelled down the hill.

"Ah! Locals," said a man with a shock of white hair. Turning to his companions, he said, "Soon sort this out now, chaps." Moving towards the sudden influx of 'locals,' the man extended his hand and spoke loudly.

Henry wondered if he was going to offer them some trade-beads.'

"WE-ARE-LOST," shouted the white haired stranger waving his hand to encompass all the people and the two coaches. He seemed to be intimating that the great white chief had sent his magic birds and these yokels might panic.

"Oh for goodness sake," said a no-nonsense voice. The crowd parted to reveal an attractive woman in a long green evening dress. She made straight for Henry and shook his hand. "Never mind him. We are looking for a gentleman named Cuthbert. A friend of mine, Geraldine, said he may be able to help us."

Henry returned her smile, "Well if Cuthbert can help it will be a first, but we will all be here to watch!"

The story unfolded as Samantha explained that they were a well known orchestra, but had lost their rehearsal hall after flash-flooding in another valley. Geraldine mentioned the huge cinema building and suggested that it might be available until repairs were made.

"Another string to your violin, eh?" quipped the Captain.

Samantha looked at him blankly. "But then it wouldn't be the same instrument at all now, would it?" she queried.

The Captain quailed under the look of utter incomprehension.

Samantha continued, "Had a bit of a tussle with the technology. The Satellite-navigation sent us up here." She shrugged helplessly and Cuthbert's heart fluttered as if the harp section had already begun to practice.

Percy was investigating rumours of technology. He climbed aboard the coach and overheard the driver telling the Captain that he had instructed his coach to take them to the 'old theatre in the Valley' and they had ended up here. The Captain walked away with him to show him the correct route, and Percy was alone with the technology.

Technology didn't faze Percy at all. It was all a bit like gardening as far as he was concerned. If you put it in the right place and ignored it for long enough, something would appear. It was these people who constantly tormented their plants who gave them a complex. *It was easier to stay in the ground than to come up and be criticised.*

Pulling himself up the steps using a well placed handle caused the door to hiss shut behind him. It wasn't obvious that the engine was running, because engines had come on a lot since Percy's tractor was made.

Percy sat in the comfortable driving seat, studied the driving cab and pulled a few things. Most of those made his seat go up, or down. One of them made him spin around. Now he tried pushing things. Air hissed out at him, first hot then cold. Music came from somewhere and eventually the whole bus seemed to lift itself up.

Percy spotted a screen built into the dashboard and tapped it. The roads looked familiar and he recognised the Valley. *This must be the thing you instruct.* It looked like a training device, so that you could practice without going anywhere.

Spotting a microphone Percy unclipped it and pressed the button. *This must be where you give the commands.* "Straight ahead," said Percy.

"STRAIGHT AHEAD," boomed out from speakers down the length of the bus. Percy frowned. *He wouldn't get far if it kept answering back.*

Lowering his seat so he could rest his feet on the pedals, Percy tried various combinations of actions. The map started to turn in front of him! This was more like it! He had seen a computer game in an arcade once, just like this. Percy beamed at the screen. The little buildings were moving around the edges and slowly disappearing behind the edge of the screen. This was fun!

The driver of the second coach almost choked on his coffee.

What was his mate doing leaving without warning him? Half the orchestra were still wandering about outside. Still, if he didn't follow he wouldn't get a hotel room with a TV. He began to manoeuvre his coach around so that he could follow.

Percy had his eyes glued to the screen in front of him, he knew that at some point the bad guys would appear and start shooting at him. They wouldn't catch Percy Plumm napping, oh no!

The crow was wheeling in circles above Cuthbert's farm. He had long ago worked out the safest height to operate was where missiles of all descriptions would fail to reach him. He sometimes wondered if the farm was a 'cover' for an experimental weapons group! Lazily riding the thermals, he watched what seemed to be two huge caterpillars slowly turning in front of the farm buildings. *If that's the caterpillar, I'd hate to see the cabbage.* He tipped one wing to get a better view, and began to descend.

The second driver watched in disbelief as suitcases and music cases began to tumble from the coach in front. It seemed to be speeding up! Reaching for his microphone, he called, "Road rider two, can you hear me?" After repeating himself several times, he turned the volume right up and yelled, "Hey you in the bus, can you hear me?"

Percy was still hunched over the screen waiting for the trap to spring; perhaps it would be a broken bridge across the river. *Concentrate Percy.* The shouted question boomed out from all the speakers in the bus and made him jump.

He looked up startled to see that Cuthbert's farm had gone and there was a crow coming straight for him! He was moving, fast!

The crow spotted Percy. After all their encounters he knew how to recognise him from any angle, day or night. Increasing his dive angle, the crow adjusted his 'air-brake' feathers and lined up on the top of Percy's head.

This was it; Percy looked up and saw the inevitable. *Somehow*, thought the crow, *he doesn't look too bothered!*

The crow hit the windscreen with a thump and slid downwards with a 'squeegee' on the glass. His last thought was *Damn weapons establishment, they've beaten us to the force-field!*

Percy instinctively threw his hands up and knocked the door lever by accident. The speakers boomed "WHERE DO YOU THINK YOU ARE GOING?"

Marvellous, thought Percy, *Now it wants to talk to me*, and he jumped!

The driver in the coach behind saw something tumbling away from the bus and thought it was suitcases, the air was full of feathers too!

He followed the bus in front, secure in the knowledge that his colleague had obtained a short cut from the locals and was making up for lost time. Why some of the orchestra had stayed behind at that dump was beyond him, but let's face it, they didn't call him 'Thinker' did they? No, they called him 'Driver,' so he drove!

The sat-nav in the second bus showed a very narrow bridge coming up, but the bus in front didn't slow down. Whomever had fitted an auto-pilot device to these buses had never met Percy. The first bus crunched into the wedge-shaped bridge and stuck. The second bus crashed into the back of it and entwined the two wrecks firmly together. The driver of the second bus climbed out and scratched his head.

The driver of the first bus ran up the road behind him. "Why did you leave me behind?" he gasped. The driver of the second bus began to calculate career choices which did not involve the word 'driver'.

Percy sauntered back to the farmhouse. Cuthbert raised an eyebrow as they passed in the kitchen.

Percy grumbled, "What's the point of putting a games machine in a bus. It's a wonder they ever get where they're going." Then he tripped over a violin case.

The table was piled high with violin cases. There was a cello, or a double bass, propped in each corner and a harp stood perilously close to the cooking range.

Cuthbert intercepted the floor level tirade from Percy and explained that the buses had gone without the orchestra and they were staying the night. Cuthbert would show them the cinema building tomorrow and they may be renting it for a while.

Percy stumped away into the far recesses of the house and Cuthbert began the process of locking up. Looking around at all the belongings scattered about the place, he wondered whether it was worth the effort. Everybody from outside seemed to be inside. Who was left to break in?

As he completed the upstairs checks and started back downstairs, he heard a sonorous bass sound, regular, rhythmic.

Heading out of the kitchen Cuthbert could just make out the shape of Percy sitting with his back to him in an armchair. Above him, was the unmistakeable shape of the tuning head of a cello.

Wonders will never cease, thought Cuthbert, *Percy is musical.*

Stepping carefully so as not to disturb the recital, Cuthbert crept forward and turned to face his friend. Percy was fast asleep leaning on the cello, snoring into the sound hole!

Chapter 13

The next morning was chaos. Men were wandering around with wires dangling from shavers and looking for sockets.

A foreign woman kept trying to plug her hair drier into the meat-mincer, and every time Cuthbert boiled the kettle someone took it outside and poured it into the bath! The table looked like the baggage claim at a major international airport and toast was flying out of the grill like someone dealing a hand at poker.

Eventually Samantha assembled the scruffiest looking orchestra on the planet and they all lugged their instruments over the hill to the cinema.

Henry and the Captain met them there and helped to arrange the seating. Cuthbert enjoyed the limelight when he showed them how much room they had to practice in. He even accepted a kiss on the cheek from Samantha.

Percy meanwhile had been given the job of transporting the heavier items by road. There was a harp and several strange shaped cylinders with curved bases. Percy chucked them all onto a trailer, which in another life had been a hay-cart, and he set off.

The crow watched from his perch on the thatch. He had been up all night trying to pick a fight with anything big enough to straighten his beak out with a good punch.

Why were badgers so hard to rile when you needed them? The scruffy little one certainly led a charmed life, but crows never forgot, or was that pigeons? He could never remember!

When Percy entered what was now referred to as the rehearsal room, he was rolling one of the strange shaped containers.

"Ach, mein Gott!" shouted someone, who rushed over and took it from him.

"You're welcome," said Percy sarcastically, and started sliding the rest across the polished floor causing pandemonium as people either leapt out of the way or grabbed one and slid away with it.

"Percy! Behave yourself!" shouted Henry. "The Timpanist is getting upset."

Percy paused in his endeavours to ask, "Tim who? Which one is he?"

Henry opened one of the containers, "Look, these are timpani."

Percy remained unimpressed.

Henry tried again, "Kettle drums?"

"Oooh!" said Percy.

As everyone busied themselves sitting, positioning or tuning, several members of the group found that they were tapping their feet. As they paid more attention, they became aware of an insistent rhythm from a single violin. The tune began to soar.

The blood stirring cadences of an Irish jig filled the room and some progressed from foot tapping to Lords of the Dance! Everyone was affected, even Cuthbert felt his ears twitch in time to the music and now the clapping began! The whole room was taking part; this was the universal appeal of music, the breaking down of language barriers, the sonic melting pot of the human race.

Boom, Boom, Bang, Boom, Boom, Bang-a, Bang.

The floor shook and eardrums went floppy to avoid the competition. The dancing stopped. The clapping stopped. This was tribal; this was the music of war! The room went suddenly silent as Günter snatched his padded 'Mallets' from Percy's hands.

The Irish jig trailed off as the Captain became conscious of the attention. The group deliberately turned their backs to Percy and applauded the Captain, who bowed in return.

Percy was dumped unceremoniously from the stage, muttering "Marvellous, it's all right when he does it!"

Percy wandered across to the brass section. Picking up a trombone he slid part of it in and out before putting it to his lips, and emitting a loud 'Parp!' before it was snatched away from him.

The lady with the violin actually wouldn't have minded him having a go, if he hadn't sat on her Stradivarius when trying to play the bongos!

The timpanist was watching him closely, so Percy edged closer to Samantha. She had made the mistake of smiling at him and so he nodded towards the watching drummer and said, "One man short of a quartet, that one."

Samantha regarded him seriously. "Oh, we never put Timpani in a quartet. That would never do! Besides, you must realise that if a man was missing then it would be a trio, and we put the Timpani into a trio even less times than we do into a quartet."

Percy studied her - this woman was the real thing, she had absolutely no sense of humour! *Where's Cuthbert?* he thought.

Cuthbert was pretending to listen to someone who needed something from him, but he was so busy watching Samantha across the room that the person gave up and went away.

Percy sidled up and stood beside Cuthbert. "Nice woman that Samantha."

Cuthbert replied with, "What do you two talk about? I can never gain her interest."

Percy looked at his friend in astonishment. "Oh it's easy. She likes a good laugh that one. And of course she loves music, so if you combine the two…"

Cuthbert beamed at his friend, "Of course, thanks Percy," and off he went, rehearsing sizzling openers to impress Samantha.

Chapter 14

Marvin sat behind his desk. The interfering cleaner had turned his name plaque around again so that it faced the door.

Two people had entered, apologised and left, already this morning. His in-tray was still empty too! Scanning the far wall Marvin saw that his list had reached the bottom, but there was no cohesion in the list; he would leave a space in between the next column so that he could add colour-coded arrows linking a person to an event. '*Yes*,' he thought, that was why he was Head of the Department instead of one of the drones out there.

It was time to contact Cuthbert again and discuss ways to promote the achievements of his office. It didn't matter that his office had only just heard about the international cemetery on its doorstep. It wasn't about self-glory or having one's photograph in the papers. It was the law of undeserved returns. Whoever alerted the media took the credit!

Cuthbert stood behind Samantha. She shouldered a violin and her hips were swivelling as she ran through a warm-up piece. Cuthbert's heart flipped as the poignant tune touched his soul. She stopped, turned, and smiled at him.

Cuthbert swallowed and said, "Glad you started first, wouldn't want to play second fiddle would we?" He grinned impishly.

Samantha lowered the instrument slowly and furrowed her brow. "Of course, as lead violinist I would never be needed to play a secondary role Cuthbert, unless my mastery of the piece was incomplete. Oh goodness, has someone said something?"

Looking around frantically, she set off looking for the chap with the white hair who kept waving his stick around. Cuthbert chewed his lip and began to listen in to the other players. He needed more sophisticated wit than this!

Marvin had arrived at the bridge to find that the valley was blocked. A huge policeman was in charge of... well, nothing!

There was no-one else there and nothing was happening. Marvin approached Constable Beeching and handed him his card. The Constable's lips moved as he read, 'Marvin Middlewick - C.L.O.S.E.D.' Returning the card, the officer commented, "Well, that's two of you then."

Marvin handed the card back to him, "Two of us what?"

The constable pushed the card back into Marvin's hand and said, "Two of you closed, the bridge is as well."

Marvin stuck his card into the front of Constable Beeching's bulging tunic, "I can see that the bridge is closed, when will it open?"

The officer removed the card and put it into Marvin's top pocket, saying, "I don't know, when will you?"

Marvin removed his card and lodged it behind the policeman's whistle chain, asking, "When will I what?"

Constable Beeching snatched the card from behind his whistle chain and planted it behind Marvin's tie pin with the rejoinder, "Open of course!"

Marvin spluttered, "I am a high ranking Local Government Official, I **never close**!" and he put his card back into Beeching's hand.

The Constable held it up, triumphantly saying, "Well you've wasted a good few pence on these, then mate!" Lodging it behind Marvin's ear, he lumbered off towards his car.

Marvin was speechless! Stepping daintily over a stream he followed the road into the Valley on foot with the card still behind his ear!

Percy was rummaging around backstage, when he noticed two men fussing over a multi-coloured spaghetti of cables leading from a partition wall all the way to the huge cinema screen.

Marching up to them as if he belonged there, Percy asked, "Is everything ready then?"

The two men clipped some ends together, stood up and handed him a stick with a thin wire running from it. "Yes mate, it's all yours. I'll switch it on and we will get out of the way."

The other man added, "Whatever you do will show on the screen so that the whole orchestra can see the baton and will follow it. It's a good job they can't see you," he added, "You don't seem to have dressed for the occasion!"

The men walked away leaving Percy with that old feeling of beginning a new adventure.

As the men left the room they pointed to the screen and gave the orchestra the thumbs up sign. The conductor didn't see them because he was trying to match his nervous breakdown to Samantha's so they could understand each other.

The rest of the orchestra took their places and watched the screen. Marvin entered and stood by Cuthbert just as the huge baton on the screen made a tentative move. A flute trilled. The baton moved to another position and the timpani rumbled out. As the baton negotiated the screen the violins swept in and the harp thrummed seductively.

"Not very musical," said Marvin.

One of the technicians behind him answered, "Chap's just getting the measure of it, they expect this until it settles in to a new conductor."

Cuthbert asked, "What happened to the old one?"

The technician shrugged.

Percy discovered that several different points on the screen set off a different instrument, and on top of that if he moved faster they played faster.

Double-checking that the timpanist actually followed the movements on the screen, Percy began. The violins swelled until the room seemed to vibrate in sympathy. The timpani rumbled into the background like a summer storm. The harp overlaid the backing with the melody of angels weeping. The timpani were called in again, commanding, booming. No-one could remember a piece where the drums had such a role. The timpanist was a vision of flailing arms and blurred hammers, the rumbling back-beat throbbed throughout the building.

The men began to loosen their ties and the ladies tried desperately to blow delinquent locks of hair from their faces.

The tubas came in, mournful, like the bellowing around an African water-hole at dusk. The cellos taunted the soul with exquisite resonance and still the timpani were called forth to drive the music with the throbbing beat of a primitive pounding heart-beat.

The audience and the orchestra watched in awe as the timpanist hammered away. The drum skins seemed to blur like disturbed water, the echoes falling over each other as the wild pace continued.

Percy swung back his arm to prepare the crescendo. And knocked the partition over! There he stood, cap askew, hair ablaze and turned down wellies tapping out the rhythm.

The music tailed off as each section became aware that the real conductor was actually standing amongst them gaping at the scene.

The timpanist was still beating out the greatest performance he had ever been given. One mallet head was smoking and the other had flown off! He saw that the orchestra was focused on something to his left and tried to see through the sweat running out of his hair.

Percy frowned as the music didn't seem to be following his baton. He had never produced that growling noise before! Glancing around he saw the members of the orchestra advancing, holding valuable instruments in ways which were designed to maim. He fled!

Cuthbert was puzzled about something. Actually, he was puzzled about several things, but his thoughts tended to clamour for attention, until one of them forced its way to the front.

At the moment, 'What on earth has Percy done now?' was battling with 'Why has the **C**ouncil **L**iaison **O**fficer **S**upervising **E**xcavations and **D**igging got a business card behind his ear?'

Marvin was puzzled too. *Why was there an orchestra here? Where had it come from, and why on earth was it going at such speed?* Glancing at Cuthbert, he doubted if the answer resided anywhere near him, so he looked for Henry.

Henry was wondering why he had ever considered himself worldly-wise. He had seen riots, wars and conflicts all over the globe, but since moving into the Valley he had never witnessed the devastation that could be wrought by one man. The frightening thing was that everyone in the Valley seemed to have the potential to cause extreme havoc with a simple "Good Morning."

Only this morning Henry had left the Mandrake Arms to search for a newspaper which actually recognised the outside world. He had shouted a cheery "Good Morning" to the passing Baker's van. The driver had pipped his horn in acknowledgement;

Blind Pugh had driven a flock of sheep into the road directly in front of the van, thinking it was the bus which he always mistook for the cattle truck. The van swerved, missed the sheep but managed to hit

Ronald who was disguised as a cow, and Henry had scuttled off into the Post Office.

Mrs. Biggle promptly covered him in a fine white powder by shouting into her compact whilst trying to call for an ambulance, and knocked her coffee all over the last newspaper on the counter.

When Henry admitted defeat and slipped out of a side door, the Baker was corralled by Blind Pugh in the village pen fold. The sheep were eating the bread scattered all over the road and a cow, cursing like an enraged mercenary, was trying to drag its back legs over a stile. *Just imagine*, he thought, *if Cuthbert and Percy ever went abroad, perhaps Beirut would still be standing. Several other major cities would be in great peril though, he had to admit.*

Cuthbert wandered across to where Marvin was engaged in conversation with Henry and the Captain. By the time he joined them Marvin seemed to have been filled in on the recent events.

Then he asked, "Where is Cuthbert?"

Henry played for time by calling to Margery and introducing his wife to Marvin. They shook hands politely, but Margery could not quell her inner woman and reached out and plucked the business card from behind Marvin's ear.

Marvin was impressed. "A woman who does conjuring tricks, how very droll." Conversation seemed to stall, so Marvin tried again, "Does anyone know where Cuthbert is?"

Margery looked him in the eye and said, "He's right beside you."

The rest of the group cringed as Marvin looked above Cuthbert, then to each side of Cuthbert and finally, right through him. "Where?" he asked perplexed.

Cuthbert adopted the simpering grin which he hadn't tried since Primary School and raised a hand. "Here," he said, self-consciously.

Marvin looked around wildly, "But where is that little chap in charge of burials who impressed me so much?"

Saying that Percy was heading downhill rapidly at the head of a vengeful column of musicians somehow didn't somehow seem to suit the occasion, so Henry simply said, "Oh, I'm afraid that Percy has left the building."

Marvin seemed reluctant to acknowledge Cuthbert as his life-line to guaranteeing his promotion and future, so Margery took a hand and steered the conversation towards things that interested her. "Do you have a wife, Mr. Middlewick?" she asked sweetly.

Marvin had been handed a glass of sparkling nothingness and he paused with it halfway to his lips. His hand trembled slightly. "Er, yes, yes there is a Mrs. Middlewick," he said reluctantly.

Margery scented blood. "Oh come now Marvin, may I call you Marvin?" She took him by the elbow in the martial arts restraining hold taught to women at birth, and purred. "Surely you don't call her Mrs. Middlewick at home?"

Marvin took a hasty sip, "Er, well actually I do." Seeing Marjorie's expression and feeling her grip tighten, he was forced to continue. "Er, my wife's name is," he took another sip, "Her name is, is, Doreeen!"

The stem of his wine glass snapped and everyone stepped back a pace. Not Margery, she was made of sterner stuff, would a shark miss the chance of a feeding frenzy?

As Elspeth appeared and fussed around picking up the glass and wiping Marvin's jacket, Margery pulled her husband to one side and asked excitedly. "Did you see that? His mouth went twice as wide as normal and his hands clenched. It was as if he was trying to strangle her with her own name!"

Henry knew better than to offer a comment, he merely watched as Elspeth picked up on the 'vulnerable male' signals and took Marvin's other elbow. "There, there dear," she said, perhaps Doreeen would like to come to a recital. "Does she like music?"

Marvin was trapped. "Oh yes," he stammered, "She sits in a chair for hours with the music on." The truth was that she sat in a chair for hours! Marvin just put the music on to keep her company!

But the women were satisfied. They had done the ground-work and 'Doreeen' would be available for interrogation. This little man would soon have no secrets. Nodding to each other in satisfaction, they released him and continued to mingle.

Henry handed Marvin a fresh drink in a sympathetic gesture of 'You never stood a chance mate' empathy, and wandered off.

Marvin had noticed that people were always surprised that he was married. He supposed that it was because, the job being his mistress, he didn't look haunted enough. Sipping his drink, he turned to scan the room. Cuthbert was still standing there complete with inane grin. Marvin swallowed and decided to make conversation. "So the chap with soil on his hands wasn't the undertaker then?"

"No," said Cuthbert, "He's a gardener."

Marvin sighed as the conversation re-ran inside his head and the word 'Swedes' jumped out at him. "So there isn't an international section in the cemetery then?" asked Marvin.

"Not yet," replied Cuthbert.

"Yet?" asked Marvin hopefully.

Cuthbert paused, "Well, as soon as someone foreign dies we can start one." The inane grin was back.

Marvin probed further, "No different section for odd religions either then?"

Cuthbert thought for a moment, shook his head but conceded that, "Some folk are buried at odd angles, that may mean something to somebody somewhere."

Marvin was tempted to look around for T.V. cameras, but he suspected that this was what passed for normal around here. Marvin was trying to visualise the excitement that his memos would have caused at national level. This scheme of his had ticked all the boxes. He had even seen the possibility that a music festival could be added to his plan. He could have claimed the whole thing as his personal regeneration scheme for the area. Local taxes could have gone up to pay for things already achieved. This was the holy grail of Local Authority thinking.

Cuthbert had been speaking, but Marvin had drifted to somewhere safe inside his head.

Marvin shook himself mentally and asked "Pardon?"

Cuthbert began again. Apparently, the cemetery was being completely re-organised.

Marvin brightened. Perhaps all was not lost yet. After accepting an offer to stay overnight at Cuthbert's and visit the site the next day, he cheered up somewhat.

Percy reached the old theatre complex, or barn as it was generally known. The only real danger he had been in was when that tubby violinist ran out of breath and realised that he could use his violin to fire sharp sticks at Percy as he increased the distance.

He had left them all behind now and he sat on the edge of the old stage swinging his legs. That had been fun but it was fairly certain that he would not be welcome in the 'rehearsal room' for a while.

The orchestra had returned grumbling amongst themselves and started packing instruments away. The majority of them were now staying at the Mandrake Arms with some being billeted around the village. No-one was lodging with Cuthbert at the moment. Marvin didn't think to wonder why.

Just before Samantha left for her comfortable room Cuthbert approached her and tried to compliment her. "Wonderful playing, Samantha," he said rolling her name around his tongue. "Be careful you don't get fiddler's elbow."

Samantha paused halfway through packing her instrument, straightened and said, "Now that's a common misconception, Cuthbert. We in fact don't consider ourselves to be fiddlers. In fact, the repetitive strain suffered by violinists affects the shoulders as much as anywhere. The finger cramps are a huge problem too..." Cuthbert tuned himself out. He was well acquainted with suffering for love, but good grief, this was for the love of suffering!

Chapter 15

As evening fell Cuthbert and Marvin made their way back to the farmhouse. Marvin was enchanted that Cuthbert had preserved the ancient cow-byre complete with its original thatch. They both fell silent when it turned out to be the house.

Inside Percy was amazed when Marvin entered and Cuthbert announced that they had a guest for the night. Everyone sat at the table with a mug of hot chocolate (it seemed to absorb the ink from Percy's pen better). Gradually as the heat from the range seeped into his bones, Marvin began to relax. They discussed gardening and this led to him divulging that his big ambition had always been to paint landscapes.

Percy pushed his hat back and stretched. "Oh, I understand that," he said. "Painting has been in my family for generations. History has seen many a Plumm sat at his easel recording everyday life for posterity." He leaned forward as if to confide. "One member of my family was in on the ground floor of the insurance industry."

Marvin peered at Percy, "But what has painting got to do with insurance?"

Percy shuffled to get comfortable and Cuthbert slithered into the other room like an eel perfecting its escape.

Percy began, "Well, my ancestor was very careful at all times and in all things. So much so, that his nickname was Prudential.

Marvin checked, "Prudential Plumm?"

Percy nodded, "That's right. He could always be found by a river or a lake. He liked to catch the reflections you see. Anyway, one of his favourite spots was a ford where the wagons used to stop in the middle for awhile to cool their axle boxes and make the wheels last longer. He was there one day when a huge hay cart came into the ford far too fast and got stuck in the mud right in the middle. Chasing behind it was a man shouting, 'Stop thief'. Well, we Plumm's have never been big violent men, so my ancestor kept his head down and continued painting. The man on the cart was a well known local second-hand cart dealer named Wain and he tried to get the horses moving to escape. The cart was stuck right in the middle and it all ended up with the rest of the village chasing Wain away and reclaiming the cart. Well, in those days, it was usually one man's word against another and court cases ended up in slanging matches. But this time, my ancestor had got the whole thing on canvas. It was the first 'Scene of Crime' picture ever taken. He called it 'Hey, Wain!' and ever after that everybody went straight to 'Prudential,' it saved sending for a Constable."

Marvin had never awoken in a strange bed before. His sleep hadn't been particularly good. Between the scratching in the walls and scratching his own neck, he seemed to remember every hour passing.

If the candle with the lines scored around it was accurate, that is. He entered the kitchen to the sound of a boiling kettle and the smell of baking. He breathed in, deeply anticipating breakfast. *This was the real country life*, he thought.

Percy nodded 'good morning' and lifted his wellies from inside the oven. Pulling them onto his feet he sat there wearing a beatific smile as the heat travelled up his legs. The smell of baking diminished.

Marvin was no longer hungry.

Chapter 16

Henry and the Captain arranged to meet the rest of them at the cemetery, and they waited patiently as Marvin, Cuthbert and Percy sauntered up the hill.

After greeting each other Marvin checked his mobile and found that he had a strong signal up here. "Better call Mrs. Middlewick, tell her not to worry."

Henry nudged Cuthbert, and asked, "Oh good idea, Noreen was it?"

Marvin was dialling and replied absently, "Doreeen, actually," his mouth stretched and he almost crushed the phone. Turning his back on them he began to mutter into his mobile.

Percy recovered from the initial shock and was practising his mimicry. Hands clenched by his sides and mouth as wide as possible he mouthed 'Doreeen' to the others behind Marvin's back. This caused him to resemble a constipated Halloween pumpkin and Henry and the Captain scrambled into the hole, trying to look busy.

Cuthbert was surveying the moonscape before him and wondering how he could sell this to Marvin as an 'improvement'.

Marvin closed his phone and turned to Cuthbert. "Now then, what is the plan Cuthbert?"

The ladies were pitching in together at the Mandrake Arms and clearing up after breakfast. Each of them had taken it in turn to mimic Marvin and his rendering of 'Doreeen', and now they were speculating upon the character of a woman who could keep her husband in that state.

"She must be huge," speculated Margery.

Belinda asked, "Does Arkle have a sister?"

The laughter echoed, punctuated by the clattering of crockery.

Geraldine paused from stacking dishes to say, "She may be a mousy little thing who spends all her time dusting." Everyone was suddenly busy with something and looking at the floor.

Elspeth broke the silence with, "Oh good heavens I hope not. What a tiresome existence."

Margery looked at her fondly, tapped her hand and said, "Yes dear, it is."

Chapter 17

The Captain and Henry stacked a few more coffins neatly inside the old reservoir and watched as Marvin climbed down to see what they were doing. The Captain leant against one of the coffins from yesterday and could have sworn that the lid moved! In fact, looking around he was convinced there should have been more of them stacked at this end.

Marvin was coming closer with the rest of them, so the Captain shrugged the feeling off. Marvin tapped the side of one of the coffins and commented on the quality of everything, but stopped speaking suddenly when the lid flew off and the corpse held a knife to his throat.

"Who are you?" growled Ronald, "MI6, CIA, Mossad or **R**evolutionary **O**rder **O**f **F**eminists, **E**specially **R**edheads?"

"**ROOFERS**?" queried the Captain.

"Splinter group," explained Ronald, "They've got blood on their nails!"

Marvin was trying to interrupt this exchange, at the same time as reviewing anti-kidnapping strategies as taught by the Department. He could only remember one of them, so that's what he did. He fainted!

When Marvin came to, Henry was propping him up into a sitting position and speaking slowly. "Sorry about that old chap. This is my brother Ronald. He likes to be careful."

Marvin focused on the friendly face and then turned to stare at someone holding a large knife, and wearing a shroud and an ingratiating grin. Desperately trying not to faint again, Marvin struggled to his feet and shook the only hand not holding a knife. "Pleased to meet you Ronald, er....?"

"Mandrake, Ronald Mandrake, for now," Ronald said mysteriously.

Marvin gasped, "The mercenary! I read your obituary in the Times."

Ronald was livid. He waved his arms furiously and ranted before stabbing the knife into a coffin lid. "Mercenary!" he yelled "Can't they get anything right? I phoned it in myself. *Missionary*, I said, *Missionary*." He grumbled darkly, "I told them they must be dead right. How can I lie low if everyone knows I am a mercenary?"

"A *dead* mercenary," Henry corrected him. "Surely that's as safe as anything else?"

Ronald calmed down and thought about it. "I suppose so, who has nicked my knife?"

The group concentrated on the spot where the knife had been. Then they concentrated on the spot where the coffin had been. No-one said a word.

Chapter 18

Samantha was brushing her hair. "That's ridiculous," she said. "He doesn't fancy me at all. He carries an unbelievable amount of musical misconceptions around with him. I am just helping with his education."

The other violinist shrugged and dropped the subject.

Samantha stared in the mirror and wondered whether she should try a different hairstyle. She was sick of catching it in the bridge of her instrument when she played. *Imagine*, she thought, *being married to Cuthbert and living in the Valley*. She watched in the mirror as a theatrical shudder ran through her. *There weren't even two different hairdressers to choose from in the village.*

*

The Valley Mafia were staked out all around the cemetery.

At a signal from Jasper the undergrowth formed itself into a copse. "What do we know about the suit?" he asked an assortment of branches and twigs.

A bush piped up with, "He left his car at the bridge, and he stayed overnight with Cuthbert and the chap who talks to the litter bin."

Jasper's bush went quiet for a moment. "What time did he arrive?"

The other bush went quiet for even longer than Jasper had.

"EGBERT? Is that you?"

"Yes, boss," muttered the other bush. "All I know is that the little hand was on its way to the top and the other one is still missing, sorry boss."

Jasper sighed. Egbert was small enough to hide almost anywhere, so he was great for surveillance work. The main problem was that he couldn't tell the time and there was a hand missing from his Mickey Mouse watch anyway! Jasper tried to replace it, but Egbert stood firm. It was a present from his Mum!

"Right men, we don't trust suits and we need to know who he is. We need his briefcase."

"Why can't we leave it to the adults?" asked a large thistle petulantly.

54

"Are you kidding?" said Jasper. "That bunch! One of them has spent the last two days dressed as a bush!" With a wave of his branch he sent his troops away and moved closer to the hole to try and eavesdrop.

"Where's the knife?" demanded Ronald.

"Where's the coffin?" asked Henry.

"Where's the exit?" wailed Marvin.

Ronald tore off his shroud like Lazarus and searched through his combat suit.

The Captain said, "I smell a rat!"

Ronald jumped and said, "What, where?"

Marvin looked at him, "I thought you were a big brave mercenary?"

Ronald put his face close to Marvin's and tried hard to think of something brave to say. "Some of them have been trained to carry explosives," he spluttered. Taking out two green chemical sticks and activating them, he peered into the downhill tunnel. Handing one stick vaguely behind him, he stated, "We're going in!"

Behind him Percy accepted the stick gratefully and promptly bit the end off thinking it was gum! Now his lips were florescent green!

Ronald snapped his chemical stick in half and held the glowing thing in front of him. Checking behind himself, he was startled to see a green 'Cheshire cat' like grin following.

Dragging Percy roughly behind him, they entered the tunnel. Percy found that if he opened his mouth his teeth joined in and beamed out in front of him.

Ronald ran ahead shouting, "Geronimo!"

Percy followed shouting, "Doreeen!"

"What did he say?" asked Marvin.

Henry and the Captain exchanged smirks, and Henry suggested, "I'm green!" to warn his colleague what colour his light was.

Marvin accepted this reluctantly.

The tunnel was rather steep. If it had been wet they would have been skiing. Percy was reduced to miming 'Doreeen' after Ronald threatened to thump him.

"Are we there yet?" asked Percy.

The tunnel levelled off and then began to climb upwards again. It also began to curve. Ronald thought he could hear voices ahead, so he used a series of hand signals to inform Percy. Then Ronald remembered that Percy wouldn't see them in the dark.

Being Percy, he wouldn't have understood them in broad daylight anyway! Ronald simply stopped until something bumped into him, then he turned and addressed Percy's teeth. "I have found a pile of coffins and there are people on the other side," he whispered. "Follow me!"

Ronald crept around the pile of wooden coffins until he was close to the shadowy forms with their backs to him. "Eeeaagh!" he screamed as he ran to attack.

Henry and Cuthbert jumped apart in surprise and Ronald ran straight between them and back down the tunnel.

Percy wandered over to see what all the shouting was about.

Henry asked, "Was that Ronald?"

Percy nodded.

Cuthbert observed, "But you went in that way," and pointed downhill.

Percy nodded again.

Cuthbert noted, "And you came out that way?" pointing uphill.

Percy nodded once more.

"Good grief man, keep nodding like that and we'll have to put a bell on your hat."

Percy stood with his hands on his hips. "I'm trying to keep my mouth shut so that my teeth don't go out," he snapped.

Henry muttered, "I knew there would be a logical explanation."

The two groups met up and compared puzzled looks. Cuthbert and Percy had entered the tunnel uphill, and Henry, the Captain and Marvin had gone downhill. They simply met in the middle! The tunnel ran around in a circle.

Henry showed the others the remains of a chemical stick. It was found on the floor giving out one last green splutter before it died. Of Ronald, there was no sign!

Up above, Jasper gave a pre-agreed whistle. All over the hillside bushes, shrubs, and large thistles, lined up into a hedgerow and sat down. After another whistle the hedgerow marched down the hill in single file. It was tea-time!

Ronald awoke in the dark. The last thing he remembered was running headlong back into the tunnel and seeing the stone lined wall coming at him in the eerie light of his chemical stick.

Dropping the stick, he put his hands up to his face and crashed straight through the wall! He found himself flat on his face in a room full of coffins. Then someone put a bag over his head.

His combat suit was full of survival gear and explosive entry devices, but before he could use any of them he had to free his hands. Shuffling around he found the edge of a coffin, turned his back to it and started sawing away at the tape holding his hands in prayer.

The group meandered down the hill. It was no good worrying about Ronald. He disappeared regularly. The time to worry was when he came back!

Marvin was very quiet. The life he had led over the last twenty-four hours was nothing like the eternity he had endured from life. His mind was spinning with possibilities. He had enemies lurking around every filing cabinet.

Even the photocopier flashed a smirk as he went by. He had met the most incompetent undertaker on the planet who tended the most chaotic cemetery in the land. There were graves that were empty. There were graves that were full. There were graves which hadn't obligingly stayed humped so no-one knew that they were there! There was even a badger set with a coffin in it! *Think Marvin*, he thought, *all those enemies and all those empty graves.*

According to the television, if you got away with a crime for a week you were in the clear because then everybody was busy with the new murder in the next episode.

Whilst Marvin trudged along deep in thought, Henry and the Captain discussed the grid pattern layout of the new cemetery and the position of the flag-pole.

Cuthbert was thinking about a trade magazine he once read. It detailed some foreign practice where bodies were put into compartments in a wall until they became skeletons. Then the bones were taken out and stored in underground rooms. In that case, Cuthbert could use the empty reservoirs and simply build a wall like a dovecote. *It could have sliding name-plates and everything.*

Percy suddenly said, "That'll never catch on, Cuthbert."

Cuthbert was alarmed, had he spoken out loud? He glanced at his friend. Percy wasn't even looking at him! Cuthbert thought hard, "It would save constant digging and one bone looks very much like another, so an assortment could be brought out for anyone who insisted on paying their last respects,"

Percy spoke again. "I'm telling you Cuthbert, that will never catch on mate."

Cuthbert's jaw dropped. The man could read his mind, nothing was safe! Cuthbert stopped and faced Percy. "How do you know until we try it, it sounds like a good idea to me."

Percy looked at him slightly bewildered and said, "Not that, *that*!" and he pointed to the farm. "Anyway, who wants to be buried in a wall?"

Cuthbert gaped at his friend's back as he walked away. Then he gaped at the carriage outside the farm. Then he gaped at the sight of Henry and the Captain stroking two jet black horses fitted out with funeral plumes.

As he got closer he could hear Percy saying, "It will never catch on you know, delivering milk in one of those. Creepy if you ask me."

The Captain was patting the flank of one of the horses, saying, "Magnificent, how utterly Gothic. I thought we had walked all the way to Transylvania for a moment!"

The horses accepted the accolades by bobbing their heads to make the ostrich feather plumes ripple above them. The carriage was a vision of brass fittings and a black gloss paint with a shine deep enough to dip a finger into.

Marvin was entranced, what was it about this Valley and death? It had provided the motive, the opportunity, a disposal site and now it had even sent its own transport!

The crackle of old parchment sounded behind them and everyone turned to greet their visitor. Cuthbert expected to see someone eating a bag of crisps but the sound came when the man breathed in deeply.

The visitor was tall. He wore a long frock coat and a shiny top hat with black ribbon hanging down the back. He was to funerals what a numbered shirt was to football; an instant tribal recognition system.

The crackle came again and the man said, "Magnificent aren't they? Allow me to introduce Donner und Blitzen, they transport the underfed to the underworld and leave absolutely no carbon footprint!" Again, there was the crackling sound.

Cuthbert looked at the two steaming heaps behind the animals and thought, *I'd have no trouble following **that** footprint.*

Percy got straight down to logistics, "How much milk can you carry in that then, mate?"

The man looked down at Percy, crackled and replied, "Oh, very droll little man, very droll!" He then gave Percy a look which left the 'little man' feeling measured, shriven and embalmed, all before the ink was wet on the invoice! "I have some business to discuss with a Cuthbert." He paused to scan the faces. "Apparently, he runs some sort of economy planting service."

Cuthbert bridled, but Henry was already politely ushering the man into Cuthbert's kitchen. By the time Cuthbert joined them, they were all sat down around the table and the kettle was empty. The man crackled and they all tensed expectantly.

"Allow me to introduce myself. It is usually too late for introductions the first time many people meet me!" He cackled contentedly to himself. "My name is Silas Deathwish and I am a Deathsmith."

Henry was a well travelled and well-read man of the world, but this was a new one to him. "Deathsmith?" he asked.

Silas chuckled and his voice turned to silk, "Yes, you have no doubt come across a blacksmith, a whitesmith and a silversmith? They deal with materials dragged from the earth and wrought in the fires of the furnace. I deal with materials which are forged in the fires of life and returned to the earth from whence they came. And I am no less of a craftsman for that!"

The assembly were riveted! *This was great stuff*, thought Henry, his inner journalist screaming for a pen.

The Captain asked suspiciously, "Would that be the Sussex branch of the Deathwish family, or further a-field?"

The undertaker's stare became reptilian. "Is there a relevance to that question?" he asked darkly.

The Captain shrugged, "Bit of a hobby of mine - names. I can't say I've ever come across yours before." He locked eyes with the man and raised an eyebrow.

Silas relaxed and offered, "Well, it's all down to an ancestor of mine."

Percy broke in, "One of my ancestors had a funny name too." He began to get comfortable, but Silas gave him a look which clearly said, *Don't you dare try that on me, little man!*

Percy shut up in mid-shuffle.

Silas Deathwish continued… "During mediaeval times lands were won and loyalties cemented by marriage or battle. My family were never big on marriage. The King of the day christened my ancestor 'Deathwish' for his prowess in battle. It seems that we have always been fascinated by death."

No-one at the table doubted him. There was something of the snake about this man. It was a feeling that if you offered a hand, it might just come back with two puncture marks on the back!

Cuthbert, the 'Economy planter' was forced to ask, "So, what do you want with me?"

Silas fixed him with his gaze and paused as if to suck out a sample of Cuthbert's soul in case he needed to recognise it again. "I hear that you are reorganising your cemetery," he said. "Most unusual, do you have the necessary permission?"

Cuthbert didn't fancy another hole in his soul, so he pointed at Marvin and said quickly, "He says I can!"

The gaze shifted to Marvin who had so far maintained a spectator's role in things. He swallowed. "I wasn't actually consulted," he blurted out and quickly handed over his card.

It fell on the table before Silas, who stared at it for awhile before commenting, "Closed?" he asked. "Does that refer to your mind or your attitude?"

Percy said, "That's an acronym that is. It means 'Clown Loose On Sunday for Entertaining and Dancing,'

Arctic stares from two sides left Percy with the impression that a glacier had just melted and run through Cuthbert's kitchen. He looked down into his wellies casually to see if the fungus was coming on alright.

Silas addressed Cuthbert, "I need more space for internments. I would like to purchase your cemetery and carry out the redevelopments. You would be rewarded, before you got to heaven." He crackled at his little religious quip.

Cuthbert was appalled! "But that would mean non-Valley folk buried there. All my family are buried there."

"Somewhere!" chirped Percy.

The assembly went silent as the offer was absorbed.

Silas waited for a while before saying, "There are very strict laws about interfering with graves. Have either of you looked into this? Also, if any coffins or remains cannot be accounted for, there are long prison terms on offer." Glancing around the room, Silas added, "I would have asked if you thought that the farm would run itself. But I can see that it probably does."

He then turned his attention to Marvin. "I would imagine that your pension is building up nicely Mr. Middlewick. Now what would happen to that if you really were *closed*?" Silas stood and surveyed the stunned faces. Percy had put his feet up on the table and was leaning back in his chair. The undertaker crackled softly and said, "I will take my leave Gentlemen. As a final word, I will relate to you my family motto ..."

Percy beat him to it. "Ashes to ashes, dust to dust, except for robots, they just rust!" he suggested.

Silas drew himself up to his full height and scoured the faces before him with a glare. "Actually," he stated flatly, "It's *Strike now, before the devil knows you're dead!*"

The room shook as the door slammed. Marvin and Cuthbert seemed to be shaking long after the man left!

Chapter 19

Ronald had been in this situation so many times that it was becoming boring. He worked industriously to fray the tape around his wrists.

The edge of the coffin was just rough enough to finally free him. Breaking another light stick, he looked around. There was another tunnel leading downhill. There was no sign of the curved tunnel he had dragged Percy through.

Moving closer to a wall, he saw that it was actually a pile of empty shoe-boxes! Pulling one out towards himself, he turned it around and gasped. The other side was disguised using papier-mâché to look like aged stone! *Ingenious*, the whole wall could be knocked down in seconds for an escape and rebuilt almost as quickly.

Muttering to himself, he analysed the clues, "Hmm, ingenious but simple - childishly simple - Blue Peter stuff - schoolroom stuff – children – school - *Valley Mafia.*"

No wonder they were hanging about up there.

He realised they had been watching this operation from the start. But why were they stealing coffins? He may have considered making a tree-house, but as his childhood was spent making explosives and attaching them to bumble-bees, it didn't occur to him! His light stick began to fade, so Ronald twisted two of his false teeth to one side and slotted a slim torch into place.

This left both hands free to throttle any demented dwarves he may come across following the tunnel!

Chapter 20

Avril sat at her desk at the Triple Echo newspaper office.

She was bored, the rest of the staff were bored. In fact, the whole Valley was bored. She had once interviewed veterans of various wars and they had all said that war was ninety-six percent waiting and four percent being terrified!

Living in the Valley was very similar. It was as if someone threw a genetic switch and the residents engaged in feverish excitement for several days over a situation which couldn't even exist anywhere else.

She stared at the familiar street through the large plate glass window and sighed. Turning her back to the view, she rearranged her pencils again and covered the spiral of her notebook with tape in case she had to interview Cuthbert. She sighed again!

As Avril turned away, two members of the orchestra came out of the Post Office. One was covered in a white powder because Mrs. Biggle had tried to call the police on her powder compact when one of them waved a piece of plastic at her instead of paying. The other was carrying a carton of washing-up-liquid which he thought his colleague had paid for.

Mrs. Biggle appeared on the pavement behind them waving an old wooden rolling-pin and calling down the wrath of heaven upon them.

The two men, thoroughly distracted, turned to reason with the irate post-mistress and failed to see the approaching nightmare vision of Silas Deathwish thundering through the village driving Donner und Blitzen hard. The horses nostrils flared, the black plumes bobbing erratically and the hooves striking sparks.

Still annoyed at that irreverent oaf Percy, Silas gave a quick 'Parp!' on an old bulb horn to clear the way.

The man carrying the carton spun round and dropped his shopping under the horses hooves. The box of washing-up liquid was pulverised and the horses and carriage disappeared in a cloud of bubbles.

Hearing the horn, Blind Pugh raced into the street and started rounding up the two musicians ready for the bus which wasn't due. The funeral coach was sliding sideways down the street, the dog was barking furiously, and the two men were running on the spot trying to get away. Bubbles covered the area and the glass sides of the coach were gleaming!

Mrs. Biggle threw the rolling pin at the men, striking one of them on the head. Blind Pugh tripped the other one, knocking him out before retrieving the rolling pin and returning it to its owner. Both men lay amongst the foam with bubbles issuing gently from their nostrils.

Silas looked at them with a professional eye. *Still breathing*, he thought, *Oh well can't have everything I suppose,* and threw them into the back of the carriage before doffing his hat to Mrs. Biggle and driving away.

Having returned the wooden rolling pin, Blind Pugh went back to his sheep-pen.

Mrs. Biggle glanced up at the sky, nodded and said, "That'll do nicely," and went back inside. A sudden gust of wind blew the last of the bubbles away across the fields and all was still.

Avril spun her chair round again and stared at the never changing street before her. "Oh well," she muttered, "At least with double-glazing I can't hear the boring silence!"

Chapter 21

The Valley Mafia was in session. The play area had traditionally been their Boardroom and now all the swings and roundabouts were occupied. Jasper paced in front of his 'men'.

"Mr. Deathwish has made his first payment. Now we can trust him. The more coffins we remove, the more we get paid. The main problem is that if we remove too many at once, even those twerps will notice. They didn't move any yesterday, so we have stopped as well. We could start digging them up ourselves, but I'm sure it's quicker if the little scruffy one gets them out and we just slide them through the false wall."

He looked at the faces, crooked collars and socks at half mast as his 'men' awaited instructions.

"We will keep up our surveillance and use the flashing light code. When we see that coming from the top of the hill, everybody get fresh branches and meet me there."

The meeting broke up and the gang began kicking each other to provide authentic bruises or their mothers would worry on bath night!

*

The orchestra grumbled whilst packing away their instruments. How could they practice without a timpanist and with one violin short?

Plus, they couldn't clean their instruments unless someone came up with some soapy stuff!

Chapter 22

Henry broke the silence around the table. They had all been thinking so hard about Silas Deathwish that they had almost conjured him back again.

"Did you notice how he stressed the matter of missing remains?" he asked. "How many of us thought that there were some coffins missing?"

Percy raised his eyebrows, "Now that you mention it. I didn't!"

The Captain asked, "Where did they go? After all, the tunnel goes round in a circle"

Henry continued, "But Ronald didn't circle back to us did he?"

Marvin looked around. This was getting complicated, but the more complicated it got, the easier it would be to hide what he was doing. It was time to assemble an arsenal of weapons.

Let the blood-letting begin!

Feeling very queasy just at the thought of it, gave him pause for thought. It never really occurred to him, that it might get messy! Then he thought of Ronald. That was it! Now he had a motive. He had a cemetery and he had an assassin.

This was exactly how it worked in the Local Authority!

The crow was never bored! He had a whole three-dimensional world to play in.

These humans were supposed to be advanced and yet they trundled along on little wheels on a flat surface - primitive! The biggest joke was that if something suddenly appeared in front of them, they simply hit it!

Swooping upwards to prove his point, he luxuriated in the warmth of the air across his feathers. A shadow fell across the crow. He blinked, this was never good news!

For a shadow to fall across him, the other item had to be *above* him! Anything above a crow was automatically highly suspect and the crow scanned the skies for a predator. The huge thing above him was really disturbing the air now. It didn't have wings like those toy birds humans sat in.

Toy birds! Humans didn't get anything right, the wings didn't even flap. This was a new one, he could see someone looking out of a window at him.

He tipped one wing and slid closer, but by entering the downdraft from the helicopter's rotor blades, he found himself hammered downwards at great speed.

Percy had wandered away from the farm. He was laid flat on his back on top of the hill. He stared long and hard at the clouds, but still couldn't summon up Cuthbert's enthusiasm for them.

They simply made him hungry! Percy's eyes suddenly shot wide open as the crow landed flat on his chest, knocking the wind out of both of them. *Marvellous*, thought Percy breathlessly, *Not content with dropping bits of birds on him, now they were going for the whole thing!*

A loud clattering filled the air and the crow was blown off Percy and sent rolling down into the Valley. One of Cuthbert's vintage haystacks disappeared into a cloud of blown straw and suddenly a man was standing where no-one had been before.

Percy shambled over to investigate and the man watched him coming closer as if he was seeing a new species. Percy was equally intrigued.

The man wore the same 'Penguin suit' as the orchestra, and his hair was slicked straight back on his head. He looked on in horror as Percy extended a hand towards him. As a professional pianist, his hands were insured for millions. Keeping them firmly by his sides, he said, "Careful, *fingers!*"

Percy looked impressed. "Pleased to meet you Mr. Fingers, I'm Percy," he said.

Having parted company with the pianist, Percy returned to the farm. Marvin had gone, but Cuthbert, Henry and the Captain were still there.

"Just met a new chap," said Percy casually. "His name is Careful Fingers. I think he's a safe cracker."

Chapter 23

Marvin was rummaging through the drawers in his kitchen. 'Doreeen' was at her mother's, sharpening her voice so that it would cut through walls and find him.

This was the ideal time to assemble an arsenal of lethal devices. He reached for the knife block. Each knife had its own slot, so that anyone would see immediately that it was missing.

He had laid out a few things already. There was a wooden mallet with pointed teeth on one end. There was a spatula which could give quite a nasty slap! As for the electric corkscrew, he scratched his head. What was he thinking? Surely, Ronald would bring his own tools? Perhaps one of those missiles which could follow someone all the way home and even stop at the traffic lights!

Somehow, watching the Discovery Channel and assembling an arsenal, weren't quite the same thing!

*

Ronald moved slowly along the tunnel. The floor still sloped downwards and he could make out scratches on the floor.

Someone had been sliding coffins this way! Further down the tunnel Ronald found coffins stacked up to one side. He must be close to the end and this is where they were loaded up for whatever purpose.

A rumbling noise from behind startled him and as he watched a section of wall began to lower, cutting off his escape back up the tunnel.

Ronald sneered, another shoe-box wall trick didn't scare him! Moving further downhill past the stacked coffins, he saw a lighter shade of darkness and knew it was the exit.

Just as he reached up to switch off his torch and leave, a barred gate closed with a resounding 'Clang.' Grabbing the bars and shaking them, Ronald realised that it was solid.

He made his way back to the barrier behind him. Adopting a stance, he pulled off a perfect round-house kick to demolish the wall without further ado. The vibration went straight up his leg, rattled his kidneys and caused him to drop his torch. The barrier was solid metal.

Someone had lowered a weir gate and cut off the tunnel. He was trapped!

The crow had rolled all the way down the hill and landed on the concreted - over lake.

Those militant Canada Geese had come a cropper when they all descended on this patch of water to steal everyone else's fish! The crow righted itself and tested its various moving parts. Of all the wonders a crow was designed to perform, rolling wasn't one of them.

Stretching his wings and giving each one a pre-flight check, he flicked his tail and declared himself airworthy. He would check the internal workings next time he saw Percy!

Hopping away from the lake a movement caught his eye, there was an arm waving but there was nothing attached to it. The crow was partial to the occasional body-part and so he hopped closer.

Cocking his head from side-to-side, he tried to take in the scene before him. There seemed to be a man in a cage! Now that was a novelty. Hopping even closer, he studied the situation. Ronald was definitely behind bars and trying to attract his attention.

Yes, mate, the boots on the other claw now. You're in a cage; let's see if you feel like singing your little heart out now! Hopping closer still, he saw that the man was offering him something.

Ronald always kept a supply of birdseed in his survival pocket in case he had to entice his dinner a little bit closer. Now he scattered some in front of the crow.

The crow looked at the seed with first one eye and then the other, and sighed. These humans, slaves to tradition they were. Do I look like a chicken? When will it occur to them to scatter a nice juicy cheeseburger instead of this pre-packaged vegetarian junk!

The next handful went over the crow's head and when he turned to look at it, he felt a sharp sting under his armpit. Spinning around sharply, he saw Ronald holding one of his vital flight feathers, grinning at him. This was a problem. Without that feather, the crow would fly round in circles until a new one grew!

Ronald shouted, "Get help or else," and then mimicked eating the feather. "Get help," he repeated and pointed towards the dopey one's farm. "Get help," shouted Ronald again.

The crow bridled, *Who does he think I am, Lassie?*

Chapter 24

Cuthbert, Henry, Percy and Marvin all sat around the table drinking tea and chatting. A knock at the door announced the arrival of the Captain, and he joined them. They sat there all engrossed in their own thoughts, and the only sound was a tapping on the door.

"What's that?" asked Percy, "Woodworm?"

Cuthbert looked around. "They don't usually knock. They are already in here!"

Henry got up and opened the door. "No sign of anybody," he said as the crow hopped over his foot.

The crow flapped up onto the table and swivelled around to see who was there. He felt his insides loosen in anticipation as he spotted Percy, and again when he saw Cuthbert. The other three he had seen around, but they hadn't actually knocked any parts off him, so they weren't seen as a threat.

Henry sat back down and he had their undivided attention.

Percy glared at the crow, "Any room in the stew-pot Cuthbert?"

The crow flapped a wing and gave him 'the bird'.

The Captain said, "You know, this is fascinating. We used all sorts of birds for sending messages. It wasn't only pigeons. Perhaps, someone has sent us a message?"

Percy suggested, "Perhaps someone has sent us dinner."

Cuthbert added, "With a free feather duster attached!"

The crow hopped closer to Cuthbert, and grabbing both lips in his beak, pressed them shut.

"Well, that's clear enough," said Henry. "I think we had better pay attention." The crow waddled up and down the table rocking from side to side.

"Looks like a flaming penguin," said Percy.

The crow nodded his head before walking to the empty place at the table and nodding towards the chair.

"He wants to sit there," said Marvin. The crow glared at him and pecked the table at the empty place.

Percy said, "He is really Cuthbert's long lost half-brother and he has come to claim his inheritance! Apparently, the table and chair are his. They were promised to him as part of his nest-egg."

He guffawed happily at his own wit until the crow squashed his lips together and sent him cross-eyed. The crow tried again. He walked up to Cuthbert and spun his head around through three hundred and sixty degrees.

"Good Lord," exclaimed the Captain, "I thought only owls could do that."

The crow nodded enthusiastically.

"It's a word, one syllable, its owl!" everyone chanted at once.

The crow shook its head. After poking Cuthbert with its beak, the crow opened its beak without a sound. Then it opened it again and said, "Twoo."

Meeting blank stares all around, the crow sighed theatrically and repeated the sequence.

Henry suddenly said, "Just a minute, owl! What comes before 'Twoo'?" The Captain twigged. "Twit," he said.

The crow rushed along the table and poked Cuthbert with his beak. Henry burst out laughing, "I think the crow has christened you twit," he said.

Cuthbert snarled, "It's better than the stuff he usually christens me with."

Percy thought it was all hilarious until he found the crow standing in front of him with a maniacal gleam in its eye.

"I've never heard a crow growl before Percy, do you two know each other?" asked the Captain.

The crow stared at Percy and then suddenly hunched over and fluffed his feathers in all directions until he resembled a hedgehog.

Henry spotted it again, "I think he knows you as the scruffy one Percy," he laughed.

The crow nodded. Percy glared.

The crow then waddled down the table and looked at the empty place again.

Henry snapped his fingers, "He's got names for us all. He thinks of Cuthbert as 'The twit' and Percy as 'The scruffy one'. But who else does he mean?"

The Captain coughed for attention, suggesting, "Well, if Ronald was here, he would be sitting in that chair, and it has to be said he does walk like a penguin!"

The crow nodded emphatically and folding one wing over his breast, he took a bow.

"Good Lord," said Henry, "He wants to take us to Ronald."

Everyone started to rise as if it was all perfectly normal to be invited out by a crow, but Percy stopped them.

"Hang on a minute," he said looking at Henry, "What is his name for you?"

Henry made a show of bending down to the crow and the crow made a show of whispering in his ear. Henry looked at the crow appreciatively and shaking him politely by the wing said, "Why, thank you."

The crow hopped onto Henry's shoulder ready to go, but Percy stopped them again. "Well?" he demanded.

Henry was suddenly coy. "Oh, I couldn't possibly tell you that!" and they all started to leave the room.

Reaching the barred iron gate of Ronald's new predicament, everyone clustered around as the captive took full credit for training the crow and teaching it to mime.

"How on earth are we going to get him out of there?" asked the Captain. "That gate looks solid."

Ronald confirmed that it was solid and well anchored. He had been trying for hours.

Cuthbert turned to Percy and asked, "Isn't that Constable Beeching's old cell door?"

Percy examined it and after confirming it, asked Ronald, "Have you tried the knob?"

Ronald exploded. He called into question Percy's height, his motivation and his ancestry. All in one long sentence without full stops.

Cuthbert let him run out of expletives before saying, "That was Percy's second home once. He tampered with it so that everything worked backwards!"

Ronald stared. There would be many embarrassments to come in life, of that he was sure, but if Percy held the secret to his plight, that would be too much! Gingerly, he reached for the knob and turned it the right way for opening, nothing. Slowly, he turned it the wrong way. The door swung open in a mockingly silent manner. Ronald stepped out. His audience was strangely hushed and very interested in the floor.

"Thanks Percy," said Ronald through gritted teeth.

The crow began pecking at Ronald's ankle and everyone watched for the bird to receive its reward.

"Oh, nearly forgot," said Ronald, sticking the feather upright on the crow's head. "There you go Hiawatha, have fun!" and he walked away.

Chapter 25

Henry was fumbling about beneath the bar. This wasn't the bit he liked about being a landlord.

The bit he liked was when he stood amongst the customers as if he were in his own front room, which in fact he was. The pipe fitting was still leaking and Henry wrapped a duster around it for now. He knew the routine. He would explain that it was a bad design and the repair was impossible, then he would watch Margery fix it in five seconds flat! Delegation they called it.

"A pint of your finest please mine host," said a silky voice from above. Henry came out from beneath the bar and straightened up. Silas Deathwish stood at the bar in his full funeral regalia and watched as Henry pulled a pint sucked through a loose pipe and an old duster. The bar was empty and Silas was intent upon making conversation. "I find it strange that a man of your breeding and experience should be tucked away in this backwater you know. Was it choice or some unforeseen circumstance?"

Henry slid the pint across to Silas and returned the stare. He had interrogated enough people for the ten o' clock news in his time. Nothing this man could ask would worry him.

"Bit of both really," he replied. "Came here for a reason, found a wife and then had no reason to leave."

He pulled himself a pint, just to be sociable. Silas somehow had the knack of breathing out just before he drank. This moved the froth away as he sipped and left him with a clean lip.

Very controlled, thought Henry. *This man calculates every movement he makes.*

Silas carefully placed his glass down exactly on the wet ring left when he picked it up. "You know, I may need someone like you when I start to develop the cemetery. It would be good to have you on board sooner rather than later." He watched Henry with the gaze of a lizard planning to snatch a fly from behind his ear.

Henry smiled, "So Cuthbert has agreed to sell it to you then?"

Silas dropped his gaze. "Not yet, but I was up all night researching the ownership details and the by-laws regarding burials and I think he could be persuaded," he smiled thinly.

Henry sipped his ale. "Up all night eh. Don't you ever sleep?"

A sharp intake of breath preceded the reply, "Oh no, sleep is just an invitation to death. It allows it to creep closer so that one day it can take you unawares!" Silas took a deep draught from his glass as if it would ward off this peril.

Henry was fascinated, "Are you afraid of death Silas?"

Silas paused and watched Henry over the rim of his glass. Lowering both his glass and his eyes, Silas replied, "Not death as such. I am afraid that death won't appreciate me enough to find me something else to do!"

Henry probed, "You mean reincarnation?"

Silas was uncomfortable, he was not used to being the one questioned. Silas looked despairingly at Henry, "Have you ever noticed that some people do nothing to earn their rewards, or that others work like the devil but it all slips away? I have studied the dead - they betray nothing and they offer no clues. But there has to be a system, a scheme, a way for an intellect like mine to preserve all that it has learnt."

Henry looked at Silas, "Ahhh."

This was a simple case of megalomania - every third world country had one and this chap had come to invade the valley. Poland was already taken.

Margery entered the bar and asked, "Have you fitted the new barrel darling?" She saw the look flit across Henry's face, sighed and said, "I'll have a look at it."

Silas drank up, put his glass on the bar, and said, "I'll be leaving. I have no leverage against a contented mind."

Chapter 26

Ronald was on his way to the village when Silas drew up beside him and offered him a lift. Ronald looked up at the high perch beside Silas and then into the back where there was only room to lie down.

Silas sighed and dismounted. Leading Donner und Blitzen by the reins he matched his pace to Ronald's. After a few minutes of silence, Silas asked, "Do you know who I am?"

Ronald replied, "The others described you, but I was engaged in an underground battle against superior odds at the time, so we didn't meet!"

Silas gave Ronald an appraising look, asking, "Was that before or after the school kiddies locked you in the tunnel?"

Ronald bridled, "What do you want?" and increased his pace.

Silas kept up easily, "I realise that you are a man of action, Ronald. I can see the souls following you. You have left much heartache behind for one man."

Ronald stopped and faced him. "One more wouldn't make much difference then, would it?" he snarled.

Silas raised a hand. "I didn't mean to offend you. The truth is that I could make you a very rich man if you join forces with me."

Ronald thought deeply as he walked. The truth was that he no longer needed money. He had hoards of it secreted all around the world, but since he moved into the Valley he didn't actually need any. He lived rent free at his brother's pub. Margery cooked all his meals. His clothing disappeared from his room regularly and returned fresh and ironed; all except his combat overalls that is. Ever since the washing machine blew-up Marjorie had made him hand-wash them.

The steady crunch of footsteps and the clop of horses hooves reminded him of the peace he had found here.

Silas broke into Ronald's reverie, "It would give me great pleasure to work with you."

Ronald stopped and looked him in the eye. "It would give you pleasure eh? Have you heard about the masochist who asked the sadist to hurt him? The sadist thought about it and then said no!"

Anger briefly crossed the face of the undertaker and he pulled the horses away without a word.

Donner und Blitzen exchanged looks which clearly said, *Dress in a jester's coat and a funny hat and they **will** all try to tell you jokes!*

Chapter 27

The Captain didn't have any time for Silas at all when he called at the old mill. He had answered the door quite red in the face and muttered something about Elspeth struggling with some buckles, before slamming it in the undertaker's face.

Silas was fuming. Divide and conquer had never failed before. These people were all simple until you wanted them to do something simple! Then they got complicated. He was running out of candidates. The scruffy one with the crow fixation was out of the question, but perhaps he could appeal to the camaraderie of the trade with Cuthbert?

Cuthbert had been feeling guilty about the crow and the way he had been treated lately, so it was quite a shock to see a giant one sitting on his stile where the other one usually sat.

Silas walked towards Cuthbert. "My," said Silas, "You look as if you have seen a ghost."

Cuthbert pulled himself together, mumbling, "Actually I thought I had seen a crow!"

Silas put an arm around Cuthbert's shoulder and steered him back towards the door. There it was again. This man hardly knew Cuthbert, but he was holding onto him while he talked. Was there an instruction book somewhere detailing this sort of method?

Cuthbert sat opposite Silas at the table and listened to the undertaker outline his vision for the Valley. *Why did outsiders always have a vision for the Valley?* The people who lived here knew that vision was restricted by the hills, so why bother to try to look any further? Silas was asking if Cuthbert would work under him. Cuthbert frowned and asked, "Would that make me the under-undertaker?"

Silas watched him carefully. Normal rules simply did not apply with this lot. "Well yes, I suppose it would," he said carefully.

Cuthbert attempted to clarify the arrangement. "So, I would be under you and the bodies would be under me?"

Silas replied slowly, "At some point they should be, yes."

Cuthbert pounced, "So, at another point they may well be above me. That would make me the under-under-undertaker and I would be three steps down from where I am now!"

Silas was wracking his brain, was there really a word for three steps below an idiot? "Cuthbert," he tried, "We are a large organisation, you would be part of the main body." He watched Cuthbert hopefully.

Cuthbert pondered. "But what part of the body would I be? I don't mind being someone's right-hand, but there's not much status in being someone else's left leg, now is there?"

There was a silence between them until Cuthbert suddenly asked, "Who is the head?"

Silas spluttered, "Well I am of course."

"So I would be the feet?"

Silas tried to be reassuring, "No, no, of course not, you would be something in the middle."

Cuthbert stared, "I don't like the sound of that."

Silas stared at a spot in-between Cuthbert's eyes. He was still staring at it after Cuthbert had gone outside to check something he couldn't remember the name of.

Eventually, some remnants of pride deep inside Silas came to his rescue and he walked back to his hearse in a daze.

Chapter 28

Marvin had sneaked back to the cemetery; it was in his own interests to discover just what was going on. All his enemies could disappear amongst all this confusion and no-one would be surprised to find an extra body or two. He shuddered and clenched his fists as he imagined carving 'Doreeen' on a headstone.

Hiding behind a bush in the twilight, Marvin watched as two of the Valley Mafia turned a large wheel. This must be raising the weir gate, he surmised. More of the Mafia were lurking on that curious concrete lake which seemed to be unique to the Valley.

He sneaked further up the hill until he came to the old reservoir where Cuthbert was storing the coffins ready for re-burial later. There was a scuffling noise, followed by a scraping sound from inside the hole, and Marvin waited for it to stop before he shone his torch downwards.

The coffins were still stacked quite high up and Marvin lowered himself onto the top of one. Climbing down further, he sat upon a coffin right at the downhill tunnel. Noises behind him caused Marvin to flatten himself on the lid in panic.

Someone said, "One good heave and we're done for tonight, if we take any off the big pile someone might notice."

Marvin felt the coffin lurch beneath him and then begin to slide! He risked switching on his torch as the coffin picked up speed. There was a solid stone wall approaching rapidly! Marvin flattened himself and by reaching down each side, grabbed the brass handles and hung on tightly.

The wall crashed about him, large stones were bouncing off him but he didn't feel a thing! The coffin picked up speed until the wind was whistling past him and the torch beam showed a pattern of stonework racing backwards around him. Suddenly he felt the wind stop and the coffin slowing down. He was outside! The coffin slowly turned as it came to a halt and someone spoke.

"Is it Marvin?" asked a silky voice.

Silas and Marvin sat side by side on the high driving seat of the horse drawn hearse. It was dark now and if Marvin looked directly at the undertaker, all he could see was a Silas-shaped black space where the stars should be!

Silas was agreeing fully with Marvin. "I understand Marvin, I really do," he was saying. "Special men walk the earth and I believe that you are one of them. That's why I came to you first."

Marvin felt a great weight lifting from him. It was partly guilt and partly blame, but it was mostly the removal of the two heavy brass handles which Silas had managed to prise from his fingers!

Marvin poured his heart out to the only person who had ever listened to him. This was a speciality unique to Silas. He recognised death when he saw it, and when dealing with the living he identified the parts which had died inside them. Usually love, ambition, and teenage arrogance! This gave him the raw materials to work with. Marvin was his man!

Watching the carriage drive slowly away Ronald adjusted the bush around him and stood. Gripping its branches firmly, he began to walk downhill.

Behind him another bush began to move, and behind that another one followed. The Valley Mafia surveillance team headed for the assembly point at the bottom of the hill. The last man watched as the others drifted downwards. Truly, the hills were alive!

Chapter 29

Avril sat at the back of the rehearsal room. She had been sent to interview Samantha for insights into the forthcoming concert.

Having absolutely no ear for music, she had no interest at all in what was going on. Samantha's lack of humour hadn't helped either. The two didn't even share the same lipstick!

Somehow Avril's journalistic spirit had died somewhat since coming to the valley. She envied Geraldine who went away on archaeological digs and came back with stories of people interacting normally with each other.

Sweeping the stage with a bored gaze, Avril suddenly focused on a man sat on a stool. His hands were held out in front, his fingers slightly clawed. But, there was nothing in front of him!

At the opposite end of the stage stood a line of gleaming 'kettle-drums' with no-one behind them. Paying a bit more attention Avril was rewarded by the sight of a violin propped up on a chair. The music was flowing, the man was waving his hands at thin air, the drums were noticeably silent and the violin wasn't even pretending it was taking part!

Avril sauntered down to the front. Now she thought about it, there were gaps in the music where everyone watched politely as the man on the stool threw his head back and jammed his hands downwards into nothing. There was also a polite wait whilst the drums didn't roll.

The orchestra took a break.

Avril sidled up to Samantha and asked, "Wouldn't that chap on the stool play the drums better if he pulled it closer to the things he should be hitting?"

Samantha's eyes widened in shock. "That man is *Il maestro,* one of the world's finest pianists. He makes the instrument part of his soul and the audience weep," she said with passion.

Avril glanced over at him, and said, "Wouldn't it be more effective if he actually had a piano?"

Samantha looked down her nose at the reporter. "There has been a problem with transport. We are enquiring into a substitute."

Avril persisted, "And the drums?"

Samantha sighed. "There has been a terrible accident," she said, "Two of our members have been injured by a vehicle of death."

Avril snorted, "That's a bit dramatic. A car is only as deadly as its driver, surely?"

Samantha stared. "I believe that I was entirely accurate in my description," she said snootily. "It was a horse-drawn hearse after all!" Adding, "And don't call me Shirley."

Avril walked away. *Only in this Valley, a question is not a question. A reply is not a reply and information only comes from the local gossip if you lean on the right five-bar gate.*

Chapter 30

Marvin was back in his office. He had sharpened his pencils and aligned his notepad with the edges of his desk.

Now he was free to revel in the opportunity offered to him by Silas. He had to admit that he was in awe of the man. The undertaker was remarkably astute. He understood all the frustrations in Marvin's life.

It was almost as if he had reached the dizzy heights of Local Authority himself!

*

Percy was bored. He didn't really want to sit in on rehearsals with the orchestra, but as soon as he couldn't it seemed like the most desirable pastime on earth!

He kicked out at a pebble almost buried in the dust and then hopped all the way to the outbuildings when he discovered that it was the top of a large rock!

The outbuildings were like an adventure playground for the terminally nosy. Throughout Cuthbert's life everything seemed to go in, but very little ever came out.

Percy considered it his duty to vet the contents personally. Climbing over an old plough and walking along the shafts of an old wagon, Percy reached an area towards the back where the items must have been the first ones in.

He banged open an old shutter to let some light in and saw Cuthbert approaching. Looking around quickly, Percy spotted a small haversack with a shoulder strap.

Grabbing it, he found an old gas mask inside. It had a rubber face with two large glass eye-holes and a rubber tube hanging down to a tin containing a filter. Fitting it over his red shock of hair, Percy manoeuvred it into place before putting his cap back on. He then stuck his head out of the small window just as Cuthbert went past.

Cuthbert was engrossed in reading a letter and glimpsed the apparition at the last minute. The head stuck out of the hole with a long rubber trunk dangling in front, two huge cow-like eyes slowly steaming up and making a sound like the rasping breath of a walrus. Cuthbert patted the thing on the head, reached into a manger and absently stuffed a hand full of straw right up Percy's nose, muttering, "Croup no better then old feller? Never mind, soon have you back in the traces," and walked on.

Percy tore the mask off his head and sneezed, covering his front with straw. *What sort of farm did Cuthbert use to run?*

*

Silas had been called to a meeting with the Valley Mafia. They were stationed all around the park playground and one of them was holding Donner und Blitzen for him.

Jasper sat on top of the litter bin to bring himself nearer to the undertaker's height.

Silas looked around in amusement. *It was like having one's own Dwarf Army.* Trying to look deadly serious, he addressed Jasper. "And what can I do for you…" 'Little man' was not spoken, but it definitely hung in the air between them.

Jasper came right to the point. "Where does the suit fit in," he demanded.

"The suit?" queried Silas, "Oh, you mean Marvin."

Jasper continued, "I thought this was an exclusive arrangement?"

Silas studied the urchin before him. He didn't like his tone, but he needed his dwarves. He forced himself to be pleasant, thinking that when dealing with children it was best to be as unctuous as possible. He positively oozed, "Of course it's exclusive. I really couldn't succeed without my… allies."

Jasper thought he had heard that 'little men' gap again and said, "Good, we wouldn't want any misunderstandings, because, although small, we actually possess a great advantage."

Silas smiled and with an edge of contempt asked, "Really, and what would that be…?"

That gap again! Jasper studied his victim for a moment, saying, "At our age, we cannot actually be held responsible for murder." He paused and glanced towards the horses being fed apples by his Mafia, "Of man, nor beast!"

Silas reacted as if he had been electrocuted. Snatching the apples from Donner und Blitzen, he leapt onto the driving board and cracked his whip. Silas forced himself to calm down.

They had thundered out of the Valley at full gallop. He had been bluffed, he knew he had. Or he was reasonably sure he had. Or he certainly hoped he had!

Chapter 31

Percy opened an old trunk. He was already festooned with finds.

He wore an empty leather ammunition bandolier across his shoulders from the Boer War. He was wearing a spiked Prussian helmet from the First World War, and a pair of flying goggles from the Second World War. Now he was looking for a Huey helicopter from the Vietnam War and he could start charging admission!

Seeing a flock of sheep run past in terror, he knew that Cuthbert must be singing as he crossed the farmyard on his way back. Slipping on a bright red Guardsman's jacket, he jumped out of the window and stood rigidly to attention. He caught the sun in his red coat, goggles and the bright brass spike on his helmet. Quivering at attention, he watched as Cuthbert cast him a glance.

"'Morning Postman," he said cheerfully, "Trouble with the bike again?" and passed by.

Percy deflated. Nobody could waste a man's efforts quite like Cuthbert.

Samantha was having difficulty. She had called into the Post Office to enquire about the accident which had left the orchestra short-handed.

Mrs. Biggle wasn't a lot of help. "Ooh! I don't know anything about an accident, dear. I was busy fighting off a gang of robbers you see. Tried to make off with my entire stock they did. Good job the late Mr. Biggle insisted I take the Post Office self-defence course when we first started. Lucky I was baking when they came in too."

Samantha tried to empathise, "A woman of your age too. A younger woman may have risked losing much more."

Mrs. Biggle looked stern, "Are you suggesting that I am no longer desirable?"

Samantha spluttered, "Oh no! I didn't mean to imply–"

Mrs. Biggle cut her off, "Good thing too. We don't imply in these parts, we two-ply, the winters are shocking!"

Samantha lost the thread and found herself asking, "Can I buy a grand piano anywhere?"

Mrs. Biggle looked around in astonishment, "I don't seem to have one. I wonder if the robbers took it. Let me phone Head Office dear." She then promptly took out her compact and covered Samantha in white powder.

Chapter 32

"Are you in there Percy?" called Cuthbert, "Dinner's ready." Not hearing a reply, Cuthbert moved on.

Percy had been startled when Cuthbert shouted into the window and he brought his head up rather suddenly. The spike on his helmet jammed into an overhead beam and the chinstrap cut off his reply.

Struggling to un-strap the helmet and running in mid-air, he suddenly fell. Whatever he landed on wasn't soft by any means and it certainly made lots of strange jangling noises when he hit it.

Percy sat up rubbing his backside. He seemed to have found a large kidney shaped coffin! Sliding off and leaving a trail in the dust, he lifted the lid.

It was full of thin wires. *Industrial cheese-grater perhaps.* Checking underneath, he realised that something was missing.

He'd seen sets of these tables before, there should be two more miniature ones underneath, that's why there was such a big space. Pushing things out of the way, he progressed to the 'wide end'. Finding a funny shaped shelf, he twiddled around and discovered that it lifted up.

"Ooooh!" said Percy.

*

Marvin stood back, he was satisfied; he had completed his list. The spidery writing now covered one entire end of his office wall and he had pulled the window blind down and written on that too.

Stepping outside into the communal pen, he noticed some disturbance amongst the cubicles. A harassed junior almost bowed at the sight of him and explained that the office in the next valley had suddenly transferred half of its workload to his Department. They seemed to have the impression that he had more time than they did.

"I want to know who is responsible for this. Bring me a list of their names!" he roared.

The junior fainted.

*

Cuthbert had been distracted all morning. He received a letter from the Graveyards Commission, praising him on his insight with respect to the re-development of the cemetery.

They were particularly impressed with the inter-denominational sections and the thoughts for the welfare of foreign would-be visitors. Apparently, there could be a sizeable grant involved.

That's why he had been looking for Percy. The sooner the work resumed, the better. Assuming that Percy had simply wandered off or found something to sulk about, Cuthbert made his way up to the cemetery. How hard could it be to operate Percy's tractor?

The sound of the tractor suddenly coming to life startled the Valley Mafia. It was another warm day and most of the bushes had been happily dozing.

Cuthbert couldn't remember that awful grinding noise when Percy operated the tractor. But he gamely pulled handles and pushed pedals until he was approaching one of the mounds. Lifting the arm as high as it would go, he opened the claw and dropped it into the earth. Scooping it all back towards him, he saw the edge of a wooden coffin appear amongst the soil.

Meaning to carry it sedately to its new resting place, Cuthbert pulled a handle. The arm shot upwards sending the coffin spinning off in front of him. Cuthbert watched in horror as the coffin struck a bush and a loud yell rent the air, "Ow!"

Cuthbert couldn't decide which could cause him the most trouble, a talking corpse, or a talking bush. He was saved the chore of investigating either when a member of the Valley Mafia crawled out rubbing his head.

"Phew!" said Cuthbert, as he pulled another lever.

The orchestra had been playing up a storm. Even the polite gaps for the missing men hadn't dampened their enthusiasm.

Suddenly, one by one they sighted the intruder and the music tailed off instrument by instrument like a deflating set of bagpipes. Percy strolled amongst them. Every member watched his progress with eyes of steel. Fingers twitched as instruments were pointed and hefted ready for battle. The only one who hadn't noticed was Il Maestro. He was too involved in playing 'air piano' until Percy dropped a hand on his shoulder.

"Wotcher, fingers!" he announced, "I've got a surprise for you mate!"

The orchestra was gradually encircling the pair as Percy whispered in the pianist's ear. Violins were being held by the neck and resting on shoulders. Trombones were being swung experimentally and everyone suddenly envied the long spike on the double bass. The crowd was closing in and the muttering became louder as they prepared to spring.

Il Maestro sprang upright. "Pianissimo," he roared, and everyone was quiet.

They all stood rooted to the spot as he grabbed Percy by the shoulders and kissed him on both cheeks. Then off they went hand in hand. The orchestra followed mutely.

Cuthbert was 'having a minute'. He had landed coffins at every point of the compass. Unfortunately, the hole wasn't near any of them.

The Valley Mafia had declared an emergency and run away, and if his eyes could be believed a flock of penguins were heading for his farm in single file! He shut off the engine and waited for his internal organs to stop vibrating.

At the outbuilding Il Maestro glared at his followers and snapped, "Stop!" He then stood aside and gestured for Percy to precede him. The orchestra gawped.

By the time Cuthbert reached the farm the orchestra was huddled together in a mass sulk, instruments at the ready in case Percy appeared.

Cuthbert was just pushing through them when he stopped dead. There was music in the air! Notes, at first tentative and playful became zestful and commanding. The orchestra grabbed barrels and boxes or simply sat on the floor. They joined in and the farm resounded to creativity. Its old rafters didn't know whether to resonate or detonate!

Percy appeared at the side of the building and he and Cuthbert wandered across to the farmhouse for a cup of tea. Cuthbert was saying, "I had forgotten all about the grand piano. It was my mothers pride and joy!"

Percy took his hat off and showed Cuthbert a clutch of eggs, "Makes a good roost as well, mate!" he said.

Chapter 33

Henry was worried. This was a shame because after his chat with Silas he had realised just how content he was in the Valley.

Then it hit him, it was the chat with Silas that worried him. Why all the fuss about some extra burial plots? It was almost certain that when the bodies started piling up the Council would release some more land. They could hardly provide everyone with a colour-coded bin now could they?

Margery caressed his shoulder as she passed by. "Not upset about the leaking barrel, are you darling? It's not your fault that evolution didn't make you a woman dear."

Henry smiled and kept his D.I.Y. strategy a secret.

He and Margery were ideally suited and there was never any malice in their teasing. He patted her hand and explained, "No dear, that undertaker tried to interest me in some scheme and it has left me unsettled."

Margery looked at her husband. "Who, Cuthbert?"

Henry laughed, "No, the real one, Silas."

Margery used her naturally arched brow to lend gravitas to the next statement. "Believe me husband, there is only one undertaker around here and we have bodies everywhere to prove it!"

Henry studied her for a moment, asking, "Don't you think he's a real undertaker?"

Margery sighed. "Don't you think he's trying a little too hard to look like an undertaker? Rather like a sixty-year old woman wearing the right clothes, so she must be a teenager!"

Henry was appalled. His instincts had always been so sharp, Margery was right. There was trouble brewing!

Kissing his wife, Henry started out for Cuthbert's farm at a run. Pacing himself as he entered the farm gate, he found that a mental soundtrack was urging him on to greater efforts. The swelling sweeping music powered him on.

The tinkling piano emphasised his scattered thoughts and the strings echoed his surging blood. Pausing to knock at Cuthbert's door, he heard the music stop to lend drama to the moment. A lone double-bass mimicked his heartbeat.

As he knocked, the soundtrack swelled around him.

He paused, *What soundtrack? This was real life!* Looking around, he spotted the orchestra swaying in rhythm as they blended every individual into a whole to achieve the sound.

Only in this Valley, it could only happen here! He entered the kitchen.

Chapter 34

Avril sat with her back to the street, practising headlines which may come in handy.

'No-one hurt in serious accident,' she wrote. 'Stranger accuses locals of staring at him,' and, 'Politician almost visited the Valley, but could see no sign of life!'

She sighed and wondered if she was really cut out for this. Behind her, a crow crossed the road with a feather stuck in its head, carrying a bow and arrow! Now, that should have appealed to her - it's not every day you see a crow walking!

Marvin was on his knees writing one of the last names just above the skirting board when his door opened.

The slight draught of air-conditioned air made him look around, only to see his own face reflected back at him from the shine on someone's shoes!

Marvin groaned; it was the Mayor. Only the Mayor was ever that immaculate. Marvin clumsily rose to his feet and faced the man who could end his career in a moment.

The mayor was gaping at the walls. Every space was covered in handwriting; it seemed to be a huge list of names. The Mayor took a step away from Marvin and checked to see that the exits were clear. *This was the work of a madman*, he thought as he took in the scope of Marvin's hate list. Marvin had sent signals in search of the receptors charged with firing up his imagination. But it wasn't a well worn road.

The Mayor found his voice. "Middlewick, I've heard about this multi-national cemetery of yours. On the face of it, it's a winner, but this..." He waved his hand across the hate list, "This worries me quite frankly!"

A distant part of Marvin's brain received a signal. A switch was thrown and inspiration dawned. "That sir, oh, that?" He smiled disarmingly as if he had been caught giving the taxpayer value for money, "That Sir ... is a memorial!"

The Mayor stood even further back. "A memorial to what?"

94

Marvin glowed, "Why a memorial to all the brave souls at the Local Authority, of course. It would be part of the new cemetery. I was trying to picture it as a roll-call of honour. A vertical wall carved with pride." His chest swelled visibly as he plucked pure fantasy from the jaws of oblivion.

The Mayor looked at the graffiti-scrawled walls in a new light. Now, only one of them saw a hate list, the other saw immortality! The Mayor swallowed and asked modestly, "Can I assume that I will be featured?"

Marvin looked him straight in the eye and promised, "Yours, Sir is the very first name, hence the space in the top left hand corner (The one Marvin couldn't reach). I took it for granted and didn't need to fill it in."

The Mayor drew himself erect and after shaking Marvin by the hand and wiping a tear from his eye, he left the office.

Marvin heard the stentorian tone of the Senior Official as he terrorised the 'pig-pens' outside.

"Nobody disturbs that man! Do I make myself clear?"

Marvin slumped down into his chair. *If I survived that, what else is there to fear?*

Chapter 35

Henry, Cuthbert and Percy, walked slowly up the hill. They had to get away from the music, it was like living on a film set. After a while you automatically synchronised your speech to the gaps in the background music.

Percy and Henry stood and gaped at the carnage at the cemetery. There were coffins angled in all directions. It resembled a giant sundial designed to be seen only from space. Cuthbert shrugged and showed them the letter offering a grant.

Henry asked, "Is that as well as a prison sentence, or instead of?"

Cuthbert muttered something about a meeting and Percy lobbed a brick at an old tree-stump.

"Ow!" said the stump, and Ronald shuffled over to join them.

As they compared notes about the mysterious Silas Deathwish, it became clear that they had all been approached and rejected him. All except Percy! The group of known patriots subtly moved away from him as he fumbled inside his welly.

When he looked up again, they were all sitting opposite him. "Oh! Charming," he said. "He didn't approach me because he knew that I could not be swayed. Solid as a boulder me! He would have wasted his time."

Ronald said, "Well exactly, Percy. What would you have done with a month in the Rocky Mountains, all expenses paid?"

Percy sneered, "That wouldn't have tempted me. I prefer somewhere stable!" Percy jumped up onto the tractor and began sorting out the mess.

Ronald and Henry counted the coffins in the old reservoir. This time, they would know if some went missing. As they worked, Henry and Ronald discussed the fact that the Captain and Marvin may have been approached. "Have to keep an eye on them," muttered Henry as they stacked another coffin.

"Mission accepted," said Ronald.

Marvin's position was unassailable. People were almost tugging their forelocks as he went past.

No-one knocked at his door. His phone did not ring. He was untouchable! Pausing at his office door, some instinct caused him to keep his hand on the handle but caused him to turn it.

All around the office, heads disappeared below partitions. One was a touch slower than the others. Marvin caught a glimpse of bottle-bottom glasses and a Charlie Chaplin moustache.

Inside his office Marvin was vaguely troubled by the glimpse of someone watching him. Had Silas decided to check on him? Doubtful, he already seemed to know everything!

Marvin picked up a random sheet of paper and went outside to the photocopier. The queue melted away before him and he placed the paper in the machine. Whilst the machine hummed and flashed, Marvin looked carefully around the large room.

Everyone seemed to be busy. Even the drinks machine was being serviced. *It was a wonder that the mechanic could even see the machine through those glasses.* "Glasses!" he said out loud and made to approach the mechanic.

A very inexperienced junior was blocking his way. The youth had something plugged into his ear and it was making a jangling sound. "Yo dude!" said the youth, "That paper is blank."

The professional in Marvin was suddenly assailed from several sides at once. He needed a word with that mechanic. He needed to swat this twerp out of the way.

But most of all, he needed to look up, "Yo dude!" to see if it belonged to an ethnic minority or was eligible for a reprimand!

"That's how we test the machine," he snarled, pushing past the youth.

Hearing, "Whoa, chill dude," behind him, he filed it away for later analysis. There was no sign of the mechanic when he reached the machine. No-one had filed a job sheet and no-one remembered it being faulty in the first place.

Marvin wandered around the cubicles like a wolf trying to intimidate the sheep. Marvin turned as he heard a plaintive wail.

"See! I told that dude that it was blank, now it doesn't work at all!"

Marvin strained to see over the cubicle tops. The mechanic, there he was, he was peering at the photocopier and rubbing his moustache.

Marvin headed back feeling like a lab rat as he wove through the maze of cubicles. One more aisle! Cannoning into the youth, Marvin landed on the ample lap of one of his secretaries.

"Oh! Mr. Middlewick," she trilled, "What would Doreen say?"

Marvin shot upright and clenching his fists snarled, "Don't you ever mention 'Doreeen!' in this office again." Then he turned the corner and slipped on a sheet of blank paper.

The mechanic had disappeared.

Chapter 36

Later that evening, Cuthbert, Percy, Henry, Ronald, and the Captain were resting. The Valley had gone from utter boredom to resembling an open-cast site! The group around the table were experiencing the fatigue of the working man.

It was definitely a trait which should belong to somebody else. The door crashed open! Marvin stood there wild-eyed. He scanned the room and slithered around the outside walls so that he could keep them all in view.

"Watching me!" he gibbered, "Everyone's watching me." He checked the corners of the room before adding, "Then they disappear."

Completing his circuit of the room he left, and the door swung shut behind him. Several tired men tried to think of some comment but it seemed to be a bit of a mystery.

Percy donned his bottle-bottom glasses and said, "These council types burn-out quickly don't they?"

Ronald smiled, "Yeah, he should chill out dude!"

Cuthbert nodded towards the expectant orchestra. "Okay Percy, you've found them a piano, now how are you going to deliver it?"

Percy rubbed his hands on an oily rag. After studying the out-building very carefully from top to bottom, he turned to where the orchestra were grouped together like a penguin's picnic watching every move he made. Giving them a double thumbs-up and receiving various gestures in return, he turned to Cuthbert.

"No idea," he said.

Il Maestro didn't know how he would get the piano delivered either. He had spent hours in the out-building with it. He had polished it and teased strange crumbly bits from in-between the keys. The chicken debris had been painstakingly removed from under the lid and he had found a custom made pull-out seat under the keyboard.

He sat upon this now and communicated with the instrument. Gently stroking the keys so as to make the wires hum in harmony, he fed his soul into the device and was rewarded with the music of passion. Pressing down on the pedals, the creak of old floorboards was lost in the intermittent bass notes as the vibration travelled down the chunky legs and into the floor.

Outside, the orchestra swayed to the sounds from the building whilst inside ... the floor collapsed!

"You can't take the roof off. What about all my treasures?" yelled Cuthbert.

Percy regarded him as Genghis Khan must have looked at the traffic warden he met outside Peking.

"Cuthbert, this is progress. You cannot stand in the way of improvement."

Cuthbert raged, "How is stealing my roof making progress?"

Percy sighed and signalled everyone to stand clear. The original plan was to haul it out by rope, but the blank looks from the orchestra at the mention of anything approaching manual labour caused him to fetch the tractor and loop a length of rope over a makeshift frame.

'Gunning' the engine to drown out Cuthbert, Percy drove away from the crowd. Every old nail in the timbers squealed like a hungry piglet until the roof gave a final scream and leapt into the air like an unglued toupee. Percy switched off the engine and sauntered over to the building where the crowd were peering into the windows.

"It's gone," shouted someone.

"There's no sign of it," shouted someone else.

"Percy!" shouted Cuthbert.

Percy gulped and spread his hands. "Well I think stage one went well, don't you?"

Il Maestro was aware of a crash but it coincided with the power of the piece he was playing, the last note he played hung in the air around him mixed with a cloud of dust. He experimented with a few scales. The acoustics were amazing, it was like being in a tunnel!

Moving seamlessly into the soporific opening bars of Swan Lake, he registered the echo accompanying him. The sound rolled along the tunnel and so did the piano.

The pianist closed his eyes and experienced the feeling of the music. He had played this piece many times but this was the first time the 'movement' had actually made his hair flow behind him. It was like flying amongst the notes as they appeared around him and burst into sound like bubbles of perfection. The increase in tempo powered him along and both he and the crescendo burst into the night rolling along the concrete lake.

Silas and the Valley Mafia paused in their labour to stare at the sight of a grand piano rolling across and into the distance before their very eyes - 'Swan Lake' sweeping before it and the concrete lake rumbling under it.

Silas shook his head. "Only in the Valley," he muttered, "Only in the Valley."

Percy was fascinated. This was the first time he had witnessed musicians in crisis. They seemed to have a code of behaviour all their own! Some of them tore off the plastic cuffs they wore and threw them on the ground. This seemed to indicate displeasure. One had begun to tear at his hair but finding it painful he pulled at someone else's! This seemed to mean indecision.

Samantha seemed to be trying to invent semaphore; her arms were waving all over the place. Then someone found a way to bring cohesion to crisis. Picking up a violin, someone sounded two urgent notes.

They seemed to Percy to suggest, "He's gone - He's gone."

A cello seemed to ask, "What do we do - What do we do?"

The trumpets blared, "We find Him - We find Him - We find Him."

The drums rolled, "Where do we go! Where do we go?" A piccolo trilled, "Follow Meee, Follow Meee."

They formed up and followed the piccolo as if it belonged to the pied piper of Hamelin. Drums beating, trumpets blaring and coat tails swinging, they headed for the lake.

Percy assumed that Cuthbert would have been thoroughly distracted by the marching band and the kettle would be on, but no! He was still moaning about his roof. In fact, he had been all along but the music had drowned him out!

Silas and the Valley Mafia had managed to work regardless of the cabaret provided by the 'rolling troubadour', but the sound of beating drums and marching feet caused them to finish off and disguise their efforts. Silas oozed off into the tree-line and several bushes were seen rolling uphill!

Percy had clambered aboard his tractor and tried his best. The rope snagged on the weathervane and then jumped free. This had launched the roof all right, but it had missed the outbuilding and landed on top of another one. This one now looked like a pagoda. Pity the orchestra hadn't been around to play the Mikado!

The Mayor was feeling apprehensive. Mr. Middlewick was obviously an inspirational Local Authority figure and he was a man who got things done.

But the report on his desk seemed to accuse Marvin of attacking a man in overalls who came to change his blotter! This cemetery was a masterpiece. It would guarantee them all a pension. But was it in the right hands?

He may have to keep an eye on Marvin!

Henry and the Captain had been counting the coffins. There was definitely something going on. With military precision they had used chalk to number them and reached thirty-six. It was obvious that someone had rubbed out number twenty-nine and written *Yes they are all ear* on the last lid.

Percy had found a new toy. He borrowed Ronald's portable radio and plugged it into his ears to muffle the sound of the tractor engine. It was working a treat.

Ronald showed him how to tune it in to any favourite programme and it had kept him amused all day. He had been shifting coffins non-stop for hours without a break. One moment he would be seen listening intently to something very important and the next he was singing away loudly.

Fortunately, the others used the tractor noise to muffle the sound of *him*!

For Ronald the temptation was too much. When Percy eventually unplugged the earpiece and went to get a drink, Ronald whispered to the others and they all followed him to the tractor.

After a few moments fiddling with the dial, Ronald held up the ear-piece and they could all hear the doleful sounds of the shipping forecast. "Dogger Bank"... "Shannon"... "Rockall"... "Roaring Forties," droned the voice. This would go on for hours!

Giggling like schoolgirls they pretended to be busy when Percy returned. Percy climbed back into his cab, waved to everyone and plugged himself back in.

The 'busy schoolgirls' watched in awe as Percy was seen to get out of the cab and strut about shunting his arms like a locomotive in slow

102

motion whilst nodding his head like a pigeon! He then climbed back in and carried on as before, howling away to himself! The trouble with Percy was that you never knew whether *you* had bluffed him or *he* had tricked you, or whether he had even noticed at all.

They only had the morning to work in as the tractor was booked all afternoon to transport the grand piano from the lake to the rehearsal room. Percy was now a vital cog in the assembly of the orchestra and he revelled in it. The musicians were icily polite to him because he was desperately needed, but the mutterings behind his back still carried all the threat of a violent soufflé.

Percy, for his part, had forgiven them completely. This was helped by the fact that he had forgotten what had happened anyway. He wandered amongst them as they rehearsed, plucking this and twanging that! The whole concept of pieces of wood and wire making noise was a simple one.

What intrigued Percy was the fact that if they were plucked, twanged, banged and strummed at the same time in the same place by the right people it all made, well, *music*!

It fell upon Samantha to gently prize Percy's fingers from the harp strings before he brought a potato out of his welly and invented a 'chipping' machine.

She gently led him to one side holding his cuff delicately with two fingers and asked if he could possibly fetch the piano now?

Percy rose to the challenge, threw a mock salute and replied, "Yes sir, right now Sarge, as sure as Bob's your uncle."

Samantha was always puzzled by this little man. "Actually, he *is* my uncle," she said pointing to the pianist, but his name's not Bob. It's *Il Maestro*!"

Percy was impressed. "You and Fingers are related? That must be handy when you need a promotion."

Samantha assured him that, "We don't have the budget for any kind of advertising or promotions, but if we did, we would probably use an agency."

Percy and Samantha looked at each other. Somehow they had strayed into a no-man's land in-between speaking and understanding.

"I'll fetch the tractor," said Percy.

The rest of the team promised to take the afternoon off and help with the piano. As Percy joined them, Ronald asked whether he wanted to borrow the radio again. "No thanks," said Percy. "I need to concentrate on this job. Thanks anyway, I picked up some useful investment tips yesterday." He climbed into the cab and put his hand on the ignition key.

Ronald looked up at him, scratched his head, and asked, "What tips?"

Percy looked Ronald in the eye and said, "I'm going to put some money into that Dogger Bank," and he switched the engine on and grinned.

Ronald's mouth was moving and his colour was changing, but not a word could be heard.

Quite a crowd had gathered around the lake to watch the event. Cuthbert noticed that even some of the bushes moved closer for a better view.

A cloud of white powder went up as Mrs. Biggle tried to ring Avril to tell her that the tractor was here.

Margery snuggled up to her husband Henry, saying, "Oh darling, I've just remembered. I saw that undertaker of yours in the library in the next valley yesterday."

Henry squeezed her waist and murmured contentedly, "Really, what did he take out, the book of the dead?"

Marjorie giggled, "He was asking for anything on Polonium. They have had to send away for it."

Henry stiffened and looked around for the others. This really wasn't the time or the place, so he relaxed slightly.

The concrete lake had taken on the air of a bullfight. The crowd was ranged around this natural amphitheatre and the combatants were in the centre. The tractor chugged breathlessly as Percy stepped down and warily circled his opponent.

The crowd held its breath.

Percy closed in cautiously and touched the wood before stepping back quickly.

The crowd roared!

Percy nimbly executed a nifty shuffle to distract his prey. In Percy's imagination, he was El Matador, and he was in his element. He imagined the fanfare and then the whole orchestra taking up the opening bars from Carmen and the crowd sighing in anticipation.

In reality, someone asked, "What's he mucking about at?" and some of the bushes wandered off.

Chapter 37

The scene in Cuthbert's kitchen that evening was one of quiet introspection. Everyone had been at the lake, but everyone had a slightly different perspective of the event.

As the Captain, Ronald, Henry, Cuthbert and Percy sat resting their heads on their hands, each one was replaying the events over and over in their minds.

Anyone with the right equipment to see the playback images floating above their heads would have been reminded of the Cannes film festival, except that these films were being shown simultaneously, in the same room, from slightly different viewpoints. Plus, unlike the films at Cannes, these were really interesting. Also, for some reason there was no sound!

Some general points were accepted as fact: Percy had mounted his tractor rather quickly after Marvin had asked for his safety certificate and enquired whether his wellies had steel toe-caps; his approach run had been rather forceful, causing the orchestra to panic and attempting to throw themselves in front of the piano.

This resulted in several musicians being scooped up into the bucket with the thing they were trying to protect. Percy could not see very much from the cab when the bucket was raised, but he could hear what he thought were yells of encouragement from somewhere. He could also see arms waving about from each side of the bucket.

Weaving from left to right to try for a better view, Percy thundered across the concrete lake. Every time he went left, the piano let out a loud 'Ching!' and every time he went right, it let out a loud 'Chang!'

There was also a constant squealing, which was odd because the piano wheels weren't touching the ground! The combination of sounds and the various signals being waved by spectators began to confuse Percy.

In desperation, he pulled a lever to tip the bucket so that he could see what was happening, but this resulted in the whole load and its passengers flying backwards over the top of the cab!

The piano landed back exactly where it had started from, except that its legs were splayed out beneath it like Bambi on ice and the keys were scattered around like teeth after a prize-fight!

The human contribution to the scene resembled a massacre of the penguins. Dinner jacketed people lay all around it groaning and trying feebly to get up.

Avril rushed over to the tractor and demanded a quote.

"Oops!" said Percy.

The group around the table had smuggled Percy out of the area and had watched from a distance as the orchestra arranged a Viking funeral for the remains.

Il Maestro had been inconsolable.

Margery quickly organised a 'Wake' at the Mandrake Arms and offered the pianist the use of the piano in the 'snug.' Every time he played 'C,' a piece of inlay dropped out and wedged two keys together. For the second time that day, 'Fingers' wept!

Henry brought the reverie to an end. He related the conversation with Margery.

"Polonium?" asked the Captain.

"That's Polish sausage," said Percy wisely.

"Baloney," said Ronald.

Percy fired back, "No, it's not, it's a sausage!"

Ronald held up his hands, "No Percy, Baloney is a Polish sausage!"

The Captain asked, "Isn't that Pepperoni?"

Henry held his head in his hands as the quorum debated absolutely nothing useful at all, he had to take control. "Quiet," he shouted. All faces turned to him. He continued in a more controlled manner. "Gentlemen, bearing in mind the fact that Polonium is used in nuclear weapons and can be found in nuclear waste, I really don't think that Silas is planning to fill our cemetery with Polish sausage, do you?"

Chapter 38

Marvin had to keep up the pretence. Silas had enrolled him to make sure that all permissions were granted to radically alter the cemetery. He would then take over from Cuthbert when Marvin eventually checked the burial records for the last few years.

Today's visit to a stonemason was part of that pretence. Marvin found the mason hunched over his work in a yard at the back of *Mister Mason, Master Mason and Son*. Marvin shook the man's dusty hand. He was quite disappointed. Somehow, he expected some elaborate ritual, not just a flabby wobble!

He then watched as the craftsman tapped out the end of an inscription with a rounded maul and a chisel. As the last chip of stone left the face of the monument, a crack opened up right across the piece. It fell into several pieces like a house of cards collapsing.

The mason stared at the wreckage, put the pieces to one side, lifted a fresh slab into place and began again.

Marvin was overwhelmed at the man's patience. Even he would have dredged up a curse at something like that! He began to make conversation as the man before him tapped away like an ambitious woodpecker. "It's a good job there are more of you, or an accident like that would halt production," he offered.

"More of what?" asked the mason.

"Well," spluttered Marvin, "More of the family."

The mason glanced sideways for a second, saying, "There's only me."

Marvin stepped back outside to check, before he pointed out … "But the sign says Mister Mason, Master Mason and Son."

"That's me," said the man, gently tapping his nose.

The pitch of Marvin's voice rose as he asked, "*All of them?*"

The mason never paused, "Yes."

Marvin tried again, "But it's obviously a mistake."

The man replied slowly for Marvin's benefit. "Mister Mason was my late father, I am also Mister Mason and I am a Master Mason and I'm his son."

Marvin mentally filed this under 'Valley aberrations' and looked around.

The constant tapping was rather soothing and he picked up the broken headstone which was no longer the focus of anyone's attention. Double-checking, he stared at the date chiselled into the marble. "This date is wrong," he stated. "It's dated thirty years ago!"

"Good Lord," muttered the mason, "Tempus fugit. It takes a while to get something just right, you know!"

He shook his head and added another layer of stone-dust dandruff to his shoulders.

Marvin gaped, "Has it taken thirty years to carve this?"

The craftsman said, "Aye, after that I've got the man who paid for it to do, and his daughter. Easy to get the names mixed up when it's a rush order you know!" The mason paused before adding, "Everyone's in such a rush. They seem to think that this is a big family firm for some reason."

Marvin calculated rapidly, and then spoke to the man. "You are the perfect man for the job, my friend. I have a very special task for you." He handed over the plans with all the dimensions and a long list of names. The mason took the papers gingerly and asked, "Is this another rush job?"

Cuthbert couldn't believe his ears. "You gave the job to whom?" he asked. "Why do you think all my graves are confused? He's thirty years behind and he daren't die because all his customers will be waiting for him!"

Marvin conceded that Cuthbert may have a point, but he also pointed out that Cuthbert's filing system almost guaranteed him a reception committee as well.

Cuthbert gulped.

The Captain smirked and suggested, "Perhaps that's what ghosts are, doomed to scour the Earth finding whichever plot Cuthbert put them into?"

Cuthbert scowled.

They stood and watched the work in progress at the cemetery until Marvin could no longer resist asking. "Why is Percy wearing a gas mask? Have his wellies become too much for him too?"

Cuthbert smiled, "He thinks the orchestra is after him, he's in disguise!"

Chapter 39

Marvin was in his office early. Today was the day when the Mayor and the sub-committee would receive his presentation. Everyone in the cubicles had been drilled to stand as one entity and chant, "Good Morning, Mister Mayor."

The fact that Marvin remembered this routine from his Primary School didn't register at all. After a final check around the room for youths or mechanics, Marvin waited in his office with the door open for an early warning. Staring at his walls and musing about the sub-committee, Marvin had a moment of panic. Grabbing his pencil, he began to write.

A commotion outside alerted him to an arrival and he stood and dusted his knees off. The Mayor approached directly up the centre aisle whilst the sub-committee divided and carried out a flanking movement around the sides. The Mayor was slightly startled by the chanting, but really hoped it would catch on!

Marvin oozed to one side and allowed his visitors to enter. They arranged themselves around the walls and faced the straggling list of names.

The Mayor cleared his throat, "Imagine, if you will," he began "Perhaps a black granite wall with the names of our heroic staff in gleaming white letters."

An opposition councillor spoke bitterly, "I see your name is at the top, Mayor."

The Mayor blushed slightly as he threw Marvin a glance, saying, "Pure coincidence my cynical friend. I am sure that the sub-committee are included too," another hard glance at Marvin. Marvin stepped up to the wall and pointed down at the bottom right-hand corner, "Of course sir, there they are." He stepped back.

The Councillor demanded, "Have those just been added?"

The Mayor took a step away from Marvin and raised an eyebrow, "Have they?"

Marvin thought quickly. "Oh good Lord, no," he said shaking his head to buy time for his thoughts to earn their keep. "It's all a matter of balance you see. The names at the beginning and at the end will be picked out in gold leaf." A trickle of sweat sent a shiver down his spine. "The purpose is to differentiate between the status and achievements of the innovators and the people who merely action the inspired projects."

The Mayor not only returned to his side, he put an arm around his shoulder. The sub-committee murmured approvingly.

The opposition councillor harrumphed and reminded people that, "It's my duty to ensure that funds are not wasted on ego trips and self aggrandisement." He harrumphed again, "Gold leaf did you say?"

Marvin nodded.

"All of us?"

Marvin nodded again and felt the Mayoral hand tighten upon his shoulder. The Mayor released Marvin and faced the assembly.

"This man," he began, nodding towards Marvin, "Has interpreted my vision perfectly. The heroes of the Local Authority have been neglected for far too long. It is possible that the cemetery will also have a separate plot for those who served the Valley so well, and perhaps the whole top of the hill where we can still look over our charges after we have passed the flame to our successors."

The Mayor's eyes glazed over as he imagined a replica of Lenin's mausoleum for himself. He opened his mouth to take even more credit for himself but was interrupted as the door slammed open and a clattering filled the room.

"Oh! Hello me ducks. Don't mind me, I'll be gone in a jiff!" The woman was dressed in a voluminous floral overall with a matching turban wrapped around her head. The turban was tied with a big knot at the front and the loose ends hung down like an exhausted bunny. In each hand she held a galvanised bucket of grey liquid and a soggy mop was tucked under her arm. Every time she turned the mop swung towards a committee member who tried to leap out of the way.

Marvin looked on in horror as the soggy mop head obliterated a swathe of names at waist height.

"What the blooming...? Who's scribbled all over me walls?" she demanded.

Marvin was fixed by a screwed-up eye. A long-term smoker, the cleaning woman was no longer allowed her vice inside public buildings but still screwed her eye up against the smoke that wasn't there.

One of the sub-committee half-heartedly tried to explain. "Actually, it's really a work of art, you know."

The cleaning lady whipped around and anointed everyone's suit with mop-sweat, and they all recoiled in horror. "No, it's not" she shrieked. "It's the work of someone with nothing better to do. That's what it is. Haven't I got enough to do around here without calling in the graffiti squad?"

The Mayor raised his hands in a placatory gesture as everyone began to sidle towards the door, "Now now, it's a matter of perspective. Rather like the Emperor's new clothes, do you see?"

The woman turned to him and the mop head swung menacingly. "The Emperor wouldn't have chucked them all over the floor if I'd been cleaning for him, I can tell you that mate. He would have set an example and hung them up or he'd have me to answer to!"

The Mayor was trying desperately to appear in charge as he said, "No, no, his clothes were invisible you see!"

The woman put her buckets and mop down, put her hands on her hips and glared. "How could I see if they were invisible? Just because I clean floors, doesn't mean that I'm stupid you know."

The mayor backed away and joined the sub-committee in their flight across the room.

Marvin attempted some humour, whispering to the Mayor, "Guess whose name won't be on there in gold?"

But it was too late, the great and the good were in full flight.

The staff in the cubicles shot to attention, but no-one had briefed them on what to chant when the Mayor left, so it was just, well, rather menacing.

Marvin's shoulders slumped. He turned to face the wrath of the cleaning woman and simply stared.

The buckets and mop were in the corner and Ronald was sat with his feet up on his desk. "Whose side are you on then, Marvin?" he asked.

Marvin slumped against the wall, wiping more names into an unintelligible smudge.

Ronald sat and watched as Marvin paced across in front of him. Every now and again he would stop and stab his finger at a name on the wall and side-track himself into a complaint about someone else.

Gradually, the picture emerged. It was one of the oldest stories in the world. Basically it went like this, "My Mother said I was wonderful and I agree. Why can't anyone else see it?"

Ronald sighed, got up and sat on the edge of the desk, indicating with a wave of his hand for Marvin to sit down.

Ronald summarised the story he had just heard and asked, "So, your answer to all this was to kill all of them?"

Marvin nodded.

Ronald asked, "Watch a lot of television do you?"

Marvin nodded again, slowly.

Ronald continued, "Not quite as easy as it looks you know mate. Just because you decide that a certain person is going to die on a certain day, doesn't mean that they agree with you and intend to co-operate." He paused and saw that Marvin was absorbing every word. "How are you going to do it? Some of those guns on TV look great, don't they? Where are you going to get one from?"

Ronald could see the enthusiasm dying in Marvin's eyes, so he pressed on. "I can tell you mate, first hand, that it's not easy. People are devils for moving for a start. How long does anyone actually stand still for? One leg needs a rest, so they slump sideways. Both legs ache, so they sit down. They suddenly remember something and change direction. They spot something in a shop window and suddenly go inside. Anyway, on TV, why don't they realise they are in danger when the music increases in tempo and becomes all dramatic?"

No reaction from Marvin, so Ronald gave up with the humour. "Seriously mate, if you can't get a gun, what do you use? Most things need you to get close and look them in the eye and are incredibly messy. Poisons are a myth! I swear that's the reason women constantly go on different diets. They are convinced that someone is feeding them small quantities of something. What did you have in mind?"

Marvin slowly opened his drawer and placed several items on the desk.

Ronald tested the ligature, it snapped! Next, came the bent rusty screwdriver,

"Blood poisoning takes some time," noted Ronald sarcastically. Ignoring assorted useless bits and bobs, Ronald picked up the wooden hammer with the spikes on. "Is this for those tender moments?" he asked.

Marvin didn't seem particularly depressed by all this and watched Ronald carefully.

Ronald picked up on this and said, "You are not really cut out for this, Marvin. What you need is someone stupid enough to do it for you!"

The lights came back on behind Marvin's eyes at this and Ronald said, "Oh!"

Henry wiped his sleeve across his forehead. He didn't really know why he did it but he had seen manual workers all over the world do it, so it seemed appropriate. "We seem to be getting on top of this, "he said.

Cuthbert straightened from his labours and sat down with the rest of them.

The lunchtime picnic was a welcome break and everyone enjoyed it, except Percy that is. He was fed up with trying to suck his drink through the rubber tube on his gas mask.

The Captain asked, "How many more do you think there are, Cuthbert?"

Cuthbert had to admit that he didn't know. "But at least we know that there is no-one on top of the hill."

"Why?" asked several voices at once.

Percy's was delayed due to travelling through the rubber tube.

Henry reached over and pulled the gas mask up over Percy's head and threw it aside.

Percy was indignant. "Hey, I had sucked my sandwich halfway up the tube!"

Cuthbert took a moment to answer. "The top of the hill is reserved for…" he paused dramatically, "The Watcher"

The Captain, Percy and Henry all exchanged glances. *This wasn't Percy*, they thought, *And he hadn't shuffled*, so they had to listen.

Cuthbert said, "According to legend, a mighty chief ruled over the Valley long ago and he is buried up there in case he is needed in times of danger."

"Why didn't he appear when Percy moved in?" quizzed the Captain.

Percy asked, "Does his tomb have a window in it?"

Cuthbert was regretting this already. "No!" he snapped. "Why?"

Percy scratched his head, "Well, if he can't see, then he can't watch, so he may as well be 'The listener'."

Henry added, "If he's got soil in his ears, he can't listen either."

Percy asked, "Did they bury a phone with him then?"

Cuthbert stared mutely at them. *May as well try to educate crows,* he thought, just as a warm substance landed on his head. "That's it, I'm done!" he shouted standing up, heading down to the farm.

Behind him, the banter continued.

"Perhaps you put a note under his door," said Percy.

"Hasn't got a door," cackled Henry and the Captain together.

"Hold the note up to his window," suggested Percy.

"Hasn't got a window," roared the two together.

"That must be a pane!" howled Percy.

Cuthbert ground his teeth all the way down the hill.

Chapter 40

The rehearsal room looked like a casualty clearing station. The cellist had a leg in plaster and was holding his instrument like a guitar.

The flautist had an arm in plaster and couldn't reach the mouthpiece. The man on the drum-kit had a wheelchair with a faulty brake, and every time he used the bass pedal he flew backwards, and Il Maestro was back to playing air piano.

Samantha looked around her and thought, *If only I had a sense of humour, we could all laugh about this!*

Jasper sauntered across to the picnic, attracted by the sound of laughter. The Valley Mafia hadn't been much in evidence lately as they were being paid by Silas, and the adults were pretending they didn't suspect. The group welcomed him and he shared a drink.

The Captain related the cause of all the laughter to Jasper and began to reminisce. "That was the thing about the Forces you know, always someone tricking someone else. You didn't feel part of it until someone made you look a right idiot."

Henry smiled indulgently and asked Jasper, "Does this new generation play pranks?"

Jasper thought for a moment, smiled, and said, "Well, there is a long running one in the Valley, but it only works when the phone box is working."

Percy looked interested, "What prank is that?"

Jasper explained that they took the phone box number down and put it on speed dial. Then a few of them would hide nearby and when someone came past, they would ring the phone in the box.

"That's not funny," sniffed Percy.

Jasper ignored him, saying, "Nine times out of ten the person passing would answer the phone. We would claim to be 'Radio Wally' and tell them that we had £10,000 to give away to the first person with the right answer to our question. When they were hooked, we would ask, *Which word means easily tricked and has eight letters?* We would give them a few seconds and then shout *Gullible!* and put the phone down."

The Captain and Henry laughed politely, but Percy was off! Falling over the gas mask, he recovered and sprinted down the hill as fast as his little legs would take him.

"Where's he going?" asked Jasper.

Henry sighed, "At a guess, he's off to phone Radio Wally!"

Cuthbert was startled when Percy crashed through the door yelling ,"Phone, phone," and dashed upstairs. Minutes later, he poked his head over the banister and shouted, "Do you have a number for Wally?"

Cuthbert asked, "Don't you keep that one in your head?"

Percy replied, "No, why?" and disappeared again.

Coming down later Percy sat at the table looking deflated.

Cuthbert put a cup of tea down in front of him and asked, "What's all this about then?"

Percy sighed, "I am so close to owning ten thousand pounds and only one word is stopping me from having it." He sighed again.

"What word is that?" asked Cuthbert.

"Gullible," said Percy with another sigh.

Cuthbert hid behind the rim of his cup.

The Night-Watch was a painting by Rembrandt. It showed a group of citizens wearing breast-plates and carrying weapons. They were preparing to patrol their streets in a slightly more pro-active role than Neighbourhood Watch. The reality of a night-watch in the Valley was far less glamorous. The cold seemed to have an unerring instinct for finding old joints.

The Captain decided that the 'chaps in the coffins' were more comfortable than him.

Ronald shushed him by radio and continued to watch. The bush that was Ronald was watching the bush which may be Jasper. If it wasn't Jasper, it might be Egbert with his one armed watch. Or it could just be a bush. Ronald sighed; no-one ever said surveillance was easy.

Percy was stretched out behind Ronald with his hands behind his head staring at the stars. *This was more like it. Cuthbert can keep his clouds, give me stars any day.*

He had been put there to keep him out of mischief. Cuthbert was with Henry and the Captain was alone. They were determined to see what the Valley Mafia were up to, ever since the last chalked message, *Told yoo they woz all ear* was found on a coffin lid.

Ronald whispered into his collar microphone. Henry and the Captain replied that all was quiet. Percy and Cuthbert hadn't been trusted with a radio since they had been caught using the static for Donald Duck impressions.

Percy hadn't been trusted with a set of multi-gadget combat overalls either. Ronald was the only one considered safe enough now, and anyway, they belonged to him, so there!

Ronald muttered to himself, "Can't understand it. Nothing has moved since the cows went home."

Percy tugged on Ronald's overall leg. "Don't do that," he hissed, "You'll set something off." He was getting annoyed and there was only Percy there to take it out on. "All I asked you to do was sit still and be quiet. Three times you've distracted me now.

"What is it?" Percy spoke quietly to the dark bush which was Ronald. "The cows are coming back," he said.

"Well whoopy-doo," hissed Ronald. "If you can't say something useful, shut up!"

The ever obedient Percy simply watched as the back half of one of the cows fell down a hole. He continued to watch as the rear end scrabbled its way out of the hole and rejoined the front end, before continuing on its way.

Tugging on Ronald's leg, he was rewarded with the sight of a bush leaping up and putting both hands around his throat.

"What is it now, you annoying nincompoop?" yelled Ronald as his hands tightened.

Percy just managed to squeak, "Nobody around here keeps cows!" The bush that was Ronald stood immediately and surveyed the area. Percy, gasping for breath reached up to Ronald for a hand to get up. Finding a handy metal ring, he pulled himself up, and they both disappeared in a cloud of red smoke.

Everyone felt sorry for Percy. Ronald had apologised twice, thus using up his annual allowance.

Henry had tut-tutted sympathetically, the Captain had patted him on the head, and Cuthbert had made him a nice cup of tea.

Percy rubbed his throat and croaked, "Don't worry about it. I'm used to it. Misunderstandings run in the family. One of my ancestors would have gone down in history, except for a misunderstanding."

The men around the kitchen table stiffened. Guilt battled with common sense, but was over-ridden by the fact that Percy's voice had almost gone.

"What happened, Percy?" asked the Captain duly.

"Well," said Percy in a clear strong voice. He shuffled and began.

Cuthbert sniffed at his tea to try and identify the throat curing ingredient, but had to give up and listen.

"You remember the Gunpowder Plot? Well, the ring-leader was a foreigner named Guido Fawkes. Now, the revolutionary committee of the time had started using the new invention of the newspaper. They found that if nothing much was happening in London they could visit the editor, feed him some propaganda and get paid for it! They needed a good revolutionary name. Guido wanted to be known as Che Guidovara, but it didn't have the right ring to it. After my ancestor Lione, convinced them that his first name meant 'like a lion,' they elected him, Lionel (The lion) Plumm. Guido was miffed as he had been the only one paid by a foreign power to put a bunch of mugs together and carry out the mission. The trouble was that they were meeting at the local Inn and a chap sat in the corner booth paused with his quill in mid-air before shouting, *What's in a name? Call a rose by any other name; it will still be a rose*, before scribbling furiously on a parchment."

"They changed his name to Rose Fawkes?" asked the Captain.

Percy glared, "No, they chose my ancestor instead."

"Rose Plumm?" asked Henry

Percy glared, "No, Lionel, he dealt in sugar."

"Sugar Plumm?" asked Cuthbert.

Percy banged his fists on the table and yelled, "Are you lot going to be educated or not?"

"On past experience, definitely not," murmured Henry.

Percy ignored him and continued, "The enterprise was set for the first of November. Everyone met at the secret tunnel entrance under the Houses of Parliament,"

"How many were there?" asked Ronald.

"About twelve," answered Percy.

"Huh! Not very secret was it?" Ronald huffed.

Percy snapped, "Well one of them would have to tell the others where it was, wouldn't they? My sugar dealing ancestor Lionel had the perfect cover for trundling about London with a cart full of barrels, so he was put in charge of fetching the gunpowder. On the night of the first of November Lionel was dead on time and the rest of the team came to unload. Unfortunately, Lionel had bought one huge barrel and it wouldn't fit into the tunnel. He had let his shopkeeper instincts take over and bought in bulk! The next night, the second of November, they all met again. This time he had bought the gunpowder in individual sacks for ramming down the cannon barrels of his Majesty's ships, there were hundreds of them. After a heated discussion and after allowing for several people with allergies, another two with bad backs and Guido's foreign fear of manual labour, they ran out of time.

On the third of November the barrels were unloaded and carried into place, only to find that they had been fitted with childproof lids and no-one could open them. They all had to be taken out again to be exchanged.

On the fourth of November, before they unloaded, the revolutionary committee's printer showed them the projected headline for tomorrow's newspaper. It read, *Westminster Wimps Whipped by Wicked Wild Plumm*.

Lionel was horrified. "How did this happen?" he demanded.

The printer checked it over by candlelight and said, "Ahh, I see what they've done, it should have been Lionel (The lion) Plumm." Giving his best apologetic printer's shrug, he used the excuse, "Early days in sensationalist journalism chaps. Wait until we've invented red ink to put on the front cover."

After a round of fisticuffs, it was cancelled again. With Lionel demanding that, "If we trust that foreign firm of printers for our publicity again, we'll end up hung, drawn and quartered. What sort of name is Guttenberg anyway?"

On the Fifth of November, everyone was there. The barrels were off-loaded and Lionel was sent into the tunnel to light the fuse so as to go down (or up) in history. After about half an hour, he came back out and asked for a fresh flint and steel to strike a spark with. An hour after that, he came out and asked for another. The stuff simply wouldn't light! Guido got really mad and started shouting something foreign before snatching the flint and running down the tunnel himself.

Meanwhile, the guards (whose card game had been disturbed by these twerps four nights in a row) heard the commotion and arrested everyone including Guido, who was still trying to light the fuse.

At the inquest, it was established that Lionel had actually brought barrels of sugar this time and so saved the kingdom. The King declared that, 'Henceforth all sugar shall be white to commemorate the beard of the man who saved Parliament."

"Did he have a white beard?" asked Henry.

"After six months in the tower waiting to be beheaded, yes!" replied Percy.

"What about brown sugar then?" the Captain asked.

"That commemorates his trousers," smirked Ronald.

Those around the table groaned, but the Captain asked, "Is that why there is a lion on syrup tins. Is that Lionel the Lion?"

It was Percy's turn to groan!

Chapter 41

Mrs. Biggle was convinced that this 'music lot' up at the rehearsal rooms were up to no good.

Some of them had just been in and bought up all her rubber tubing. She let them leave the Post Office and carried out her duty as a citizen. Taking out her compact, she blew a cloud of powder towards the newspaper office to alert the media. As it happened, Avril was next in the queue.

"My, that was quick," said Mrs. Biggle looking at her compact admiringly.

Samantha was delighted with the result. She had sent two of the orchestra out to find lengths of rubber tubing.

One piece was attached to the mouthpiece on the flute and the other end between the flautist's lips. Another piece was attached to the trombonists slide, so that it would return when he nodded his head, and the rest was wrapped all the way around the drum kit and the wheelchair to keep it all in place.

Standing before her handiwork, Samantha scanned the men securely tied to their instruments, stretched a piece of rubber taut and said passionately, "Right boys, I want to hear you *Fortissimo...fortissimo*, oh, can I help you Constable?"

Constable Beeching was nobody's fool. He had followed up on Mrs. Biggles' report and Avril's suspicions and was standing behind Samantha just in time to see her tying several men up and screaming at them.

Now, when a hysterical woman resorted to screaming foreign words at you, it meant that she had something to hide! He had tucked Samantha under his arm and carried her out to the car.

The orchestra would have tried to rescue her, but she had tied most of them up!

All the way to the Police station, sitting amongst the empty pizza cartons, Samantha pleaded her innocence. The Constable gruffly ordered her to be quiet, because he needed to hear his radio. It sounded suspiciously like the cricket to Samantha.

Alone in the back with only her violin bow for company, Samantha tried to work out how it had all gone wrong in such a spectacular fashion. Her conclusion ...? It was this Valley, it could only happen in *this* Valley ...!

The cell wasn't very impressive at all. It was one of two and the other one had no door. Constable Beeching explained that Percy was always escaping from that one, so he had sold the door and stopped arresting him, so it wouldn't happen again.

Samantha asked him why he hadn't put Percy in the cell which still had a door. The Constable seemed lost for an answer and pretended to take a call on his radio. However, since he had left it in the car, he was talking to his collar badge.

Samantha sighed and after sitting on the edge of the bed began to idly draw her violin bow across one of the bars. *Good heavens* she thought, *A Perfect G*, moving down the bar produced an 'A'. Samantha experimented until she found that she could practice in her cell. With a bit of 'bar hopping,' she could cover the whole range. *Nothing unusual really,* she thought, *after all music was arranged in bars!*

She began to play a plaintive piece about Russian peasant farmers slaving over a hot steppe to eke a living. *Why were all traditional Russian tunes so depressing*, she wondered. Glancing through the bars, Samantha noticed that Constable Beeching's shoulders were heaving as he sobbed to the music.

"Are you alright?" she asked slowing down slightly.

The Constable waved a hand vaguely, "Yes, yes!" he said sobbing softly. "I am a big fan of that music and my mother was a huge one."

Samantha almost stopped playing as she visualised Constable Beeching as big and the mother as huge, the Constable could take no more and he left, drying his eyes on his sleeves.

Samantha played on. At one point she noticed that the bolt holding the door shut was sliding back. It must be the vibration!

Experimenting, Samantha found that Strauss had no effect and Mahler started sending it back in! Tchaikovsky was the answer. With the strains of Swan Lake the bolt eased its way open as smoothly as if designed that way.

Well, thought Samantha, *If all else fails, perhaps I can find a job tuning cell doors.* Closing the door behind her and bolting it, she left the building!

Outside, Samantha was met by a worried deputation. Some of the orchestra had rounded up Cuthbert, Percy, Henry, Ronald and the Captain.

Henry explained, "It was all a misunderstanding. Someone had misunderstood and given the Valley a policeman!"

Samantha stared at Ronald, asking, "What are you doing with one of our bassoons?"

Ronald gave her a puzzled look, saying, "This? This is a rocket launcher dear. We were going to get you out in a flash!" All the military types found this most amusing.

Samantha fixed him with a look, "Wouldn't the percussive effect, the heat and flying shrapnel, have actually put me in more danger than ever? Not to mention the rapid change in barometric pressure?"

Ronald suddenly wished that it *had* been a bassoon. Then he wished that he had fired the thing!

As they escorted Samantha back to the rehearsal room, Cuthbert was trying to think of something heroic he could mention to impress her.

The best he could come up with was, "How did you get out without me storming the place single handed?"

Samantha explained that the dulcet tones of Swan Lake had enticed the metal bolt to open. "It was a musical miracle," she said.

Percy sniffed, "Huh! I've been in that one. The third verse of *I knew a young maid from Nantucket*, usually works for it!"

Samantha was intrigued, "Perhaps it's the same tune. How does it go?"

The rest of the crowd were appalled as Percy and Samantha walked ahead arm in arm trying to compare the two masterpieces.

Angling off in a different direction, they could hear Percy sing, "There was a young maid from Nantucket. She had something good, so she shook it. Dum-De Dum, never can remember the next bit."

Samantha suggested, "Something to do with a bucket?"

"Could be!" said Percy and as the distance increased, so their voices faded.

Ronald asked everyone in general, "What happens when the giant plod comes back?"

123

"Oh, don't worry," said Cuthbert. "Very logical is Beeching. If there is no-one in his cell tomorrow, then he obviously didn't arrest anyone."

Chapter 42

Cuthbert was alone in the kitchen when Percy came home. Percy was unusually quiet and wore a dazed expression. Cuthbert couldn't help but gloat, "Ha! I knew it, slapped your face didn't she! Serves you right Percy,"

Percy came out of his daze and replied, "No it wasn't that."

Cuthbert paused. "Well, what was it then?"

Percy scratched his ear in disbelief. "She taught me two verses, I didn't know," he said with a grin.

Henry had organised an expedition. He had taken Cuthbert, Percy, Ronald and the Captain into the next valley to visit the library.

As Henry researched Polonium alongside other related topics, Ronald, still in disguise, due to his untimely fictional demise, checked through news reports to see if anyone had missed him.

The Captain appointed himself 'War critic' and was reading through military histories. This was punctuated by cries of "Balderdash! He wasn't even there. He would take the credit for freeing Iceland after the glaciers retreated, if he could, never did like the chap," and another book was launched into the children's play area.

Cuthbert had heard about computers, but he couldn't see the appeal as all this one did was argue with him; every time he entered a search word the screen asked, *Did you mean?* and offered him something else.

How they could offer him four hundred million results for 'Intestinal tract worm deficit in pantomime cows' was beyond him.

His main problem was that people insisted upon interfering. Computers were meant to be logical and so was Cuthbert. Every time he was instructed to 'Open new window,' he did. But the blasted librarian followed him around closing them again. No wonder people spent hours sitting in front of the things!

Percy was having fun. Every time an unsuspecting customer pulled a book from a shelf there was Percy! He spent ages guessing what books a particular person was going for and then positioned himself on the other side of the shelf; ready to grin through the gap. He had already been warned twice.

Percy was eventually thrown out for pestering people at random and trying to show them interesting tractor parts in the books he had found. This was all a mistake, he had simply forgotten what disguise Ronald was using so he tried everybody in turn.

The Captain was thrown out after a woman complained about the violent books left out for her toddler in the play area, and Cuthbert was shown the door before everyone caught pneumonia.

Ronald decided to leave because his false beard was peeling off in the heat and mothers were pulling their children away from him.

At least Henry achieved his aim and they all met in a coffee bar. Sitting around Cuthbert's table with a mug, each began to seem incredibly simple after this little exercise. Henry was the last to arrive. The 'gang' were at an outside table and already had their drinks.

Ronald lifted the table and moved it to make room for his brother. Unfortunately, when he put it back down, one of the legs went into Percy's welly. Now Percy was fascinated by the huge chrome machine behind the counter; it sounded like the steam trains from his childhood, so he leapt up to get Henry a drink. The table leapt up with him and suddenly Lionel (The lion's) trousers were back in fashion.

Sulking at the counter, Percy ordered replacement coffees and watched as the beans were poured into the top. He was delighted as the machine whooshed, gurgled, chomped and coughed. He wasn't so thrilled when he saw how much came out. The girl behind the counter handed him a steaming thimble and began to prepare another. Soon five thimbles were steaming expectantly in front of Percy.

"Is that it?" he asked.

The girl smiled politely, "Did sir require doubles?"

Percy nodded and turned to give a thumbs-up to the table outside, this was more like it.

After a moment, the girl handed him exactly the same cups but with much darker contents. Percy decided that the huge chrome harmonium was faulty and walked around the counter to confront the machine.

The girl backed off in terror, normal people didn't want to be this side of the counter, ever!

Percy began to fiddle with knobs and lift lids. A jet of brown hot liquid shot up his sleeve and a jet of steam whooshed past him to melt all the packaging on the biscuits. He jumped as his hat was steam cleaned and upset a large basket of bread rolls to send them scattering across the floor. The next lever set off the grinder, sending Ronald and the Captain diving to the floor thinking that the tanks were coming.

The machine gave one last groan accompanied by a sigh, and thick treacle ran out from underneath it.

Percy grunted, "Just as I thought," he said to the room, "It's faulty!"

Stopping to catch their breath, several streets away the group looked at each other. Percy was chewing on a packet of biscuits through its fused packaging and seemed to have forgotten all about well.... everything!

Henry looked around his group and commented, "Now I know why you lot never leave the Valley!"

Chapter 43

In their absence work was speeding up in the Valley. Silas was constantly ferrying coffins away as the Valley Mafia sent them sliding down the tunnel to the concrete lake. It no longer mattered if anyone noticed that coffins were missing, Silas was ready to make his move.

Marvin was just about to leave home. 'Doreeen' had been particularly shrill this morning. She was 'tired of this' and 'tired of that'. So Marvin assured her that he was organising something so that she could have a good long rest.

The letter had been on his doormat. It was anonymous, but it was edged in black and there were horse hoof prints all along his new drive, he guessed that Silas had delivered it by hand.

Apparently, if he checked the cemetery, he would find huge discrepancies in the amount of coffins Cuthbert was claiming to re-inter. This should show a level of incompetence which would force the Local Authority to demand that the cemetery be transferred to another (Un-named) operator, who would rectify everything.

Hmm, thought Marvin, *The timing isn't quite right. By the time Ronald has completed his task there will be more than enough coffins to cover Cuthbert's needs.'*

The 'Kitchen Cabinet' was once again in session. Jasper was there, but he was wary because of the secrets he was covering up.

Percy was sulking after Ronald dubbed him 'The Wally in the Wellies,' after the coffee incident.

Henry addressed them. "According to my research, Polonium is a very rare and unstable element. It can only be handled legally by well established firms with access to stable underground storage. Old salt mines for instance." Henry paused, "My contacts tell me that if Silas is prepared to handle Polonium, he will be paid a King's ransom. He will also be likely to offer storage for Uranium and Cobalt rods." Pausing again, he surveyed the assembly. "Gentleman, Silas wants the cemetery and the tunnel system for storing nuclear waste!"

Cuthbert sniffed, "Well he can't have it. It's mine"

Henry shook his head, "Thanks to our young friend here," said Henry pointing at a pale Jasper. "Silas can report loads of missing coffins and offer himself as the man to re-organise the whole area. Then he can secretly begin storing radioactive waste without anyone knowing."

All eyes swivelled to Jasper who gave his best 'I'm only a kid!' shrug.

Everyone was quietly absorbing the facts when Percy said. "Phew, at least we stopped him storing Polish sausages."

The knock at the door surprised everybody except Ronald who got up to answer it.

Marvin came in flapping his coat like an angry gannet. "Doesn't anyone know who owns those buses blocking the bridge?" he snorted. "They should have been gone by now!" He stopped in mid-flap, glanced around the room and addressed Ronald, "I thought this was a private meeting?"

Ronald pulled out a chair for him and said, "It is. Nothing will go any further than this lot."

Marvin sat down reluctantly. Ronald nodded to his brother and Henry repeated the information that he had collected.

Before Marvin could speak, Ronald said, "On top of all this, Marvin here wants me to get rid of all his enemies and lose them in the chaos of Cuthbert's cemetery. It would be a close run thing because Marvin has more enemies than we have plots."

Marvin thought about denying everything and denouncing Ronald as a deluded dead mercenary. But, as he was sitting beside him, it didn't seem wise. He simply sat still and watched the others.

Percy looked across at Marvin and asked, "Does that include Doreeen?" His fists were clenched and his mouth was as wide as he could make it.

"Good Lord!" said Marvin, "Do you know her?"

Ideas were called for and Percy was banned from participating. It was obvious that they could not allow a massacre of the entire Local Authority workers.

Yes, it would be months before anyone noticed, but 'A chap had to make a stand somewhere,' as the Captain pointed out. If the cemetery was re-organised properly and looked the part, that would stop Silas having grounds for taking over. That meant retrieving all the coffins and putting them back as if someone actually knew who they all were. If Silas didn't have the cemetery, then he didn't have anywhere to store the waste, so that problem would go away.

That just left Marvin!

Percy slammed a fresh cup of something scalding hot in front of them all and sat back down.

"Anyone heard of the phantom chickens of old London town?" he asked.

The change of subject caught everyone by surprise and Marvin was inexperienced enough to say, "No, what were they?"

Percy shuffled, "Back in the past, one of my relatives was a famous actor. His best friend was the King. Now, my relative had a bit of a drink problem. Basically, the problem was that he couldn't get enough! Fortunately for him, the King had the same problem. They met backstage after a performance and really hit it off. The most fun they had was to set off on three day Benders, get blind drunk and then sleep it off. Trouble was; London in those days was a bit strait-laced and not very big. An actor could get away with it but not a King. My relative hit upon the idea of them both dressing as chickens. That way no-one would know who they were. They cleverly let slip to the Police that the King would occasionally dress as a chicken to check up on his subjects and a contribution would be made to the Police committee so that any six foot chicken was pretty much safe in London after nine o' clock at night if it smelled of alcohol. So that the King would not be found out, my relative would follow discreetly behind and if anyone approached, the King would dive into a doorway and another chicken would appear to run in the opposite direction. This worked for months and the two established the legend of the phantom chickens. Of course, the Police daren't arrest anyone in case they got the King by mistake."

Cuthbert raised his head from the table and asked wearily, "What happened then Percy?"

Percy shuffled again and carried on, "Well, everything went well until my relative was to play the star role at a premiere for all the crowned heads of Europe. This was the pinnacle of his career and it would introduce the King as a serious patron of the arts. The night came and the two of them were well lubricated when they cut short their adventure, but had cut it rather fine by the time they reached the theatre. When the National Anthem played, all the crowned heads of Europe stood and bowed to the royal box, but in the royal box were two chickens! It was a scandal. To make it worse, the music began and my relative nudged the King and said, "You'll love this bit. This is where I come on and …Oooops!"

Henry actually applauded!

"Brilliant Percy," he said.

Everyone at the table looked at him in amazement, especially Percy. Henry continued excitedly, "Don't you see? Percy is saying that we stage a diversion. Plant a red herring. Distract everyone from the truth to give us time to put everything right. Bravo Percy!"

The others slowly joined in the applause and Percy sat bashfully swinging his little legs.

Cuthbert nudged him and hissed, "What have you done now?"

Percy peered out from under his cap and said, "I have absolutely no idea!"

Henry was pacing furiously. "We need Marvin to authorise the work on the cemetery, to reassure the Authorities that work is in progress and that we know what we're doing. He can also block Silas from sabotaging us at the 'Paper Trail' level."

Patting Marvin on the shoulder gave the impression that the Godfather had just granted him a reprieve. "But Marvin has serious issues with his staff, wife, friends and bosses. We need to distract them from him so that Marvin can concentrate. This is where Percy's genius comes in," said Henry.

Percy squirmed uncomfortably, whining, "Where the blazes will I get chicken suits from at this time of night?"

The Mayor had been in secret talks. This cemetery scheme pressed all the right buttons. The Local Authority had been stagnating. They had become simply a system to organise things for the public.

If that idea ever caught on, some bright spark would replace them with a team of volunteer pensioners! The Mayor was preparing his route ahead, politics! That's where the expenses lay. Something like this would make him look like a cross between Oliver Cromwell and Fidel Castro, without the violence or the beard of course.

Part of Henry's formulating plan was to accompany Marvin to his office the next day. Marvin introduced Henry to the staff and Henry interviewed each 'sheep pen' in turn. He was introduced as an 'Efficiency expert."

A dying breed, thought Henry, but this lot seemed to accept the need.

The first person was in charge of writing paper. The second person was in charge of plain paper. The third person was in charge of photocopying paper. The fourth person was in charge of blotting paper. Henry's head was spinning. He asked, "Who is in charge of ink-blots?"

Marvin was affronted, "We no longer use antiquated ink in this state of the art department."

The 'blotting paper operative' looked down sheepishly and Henry moved on.

Back in Marvin's office, Henry tried hard not to stare at the walls. It was like a cell in Broadmoor, but without the security. He was slightly unnerved by the smudged letters, where someone seemed to have slid to the floor! Marvin waited for his assessment.

Henry began, "This Department could be cut by a third and then reconsolidated into one good secretary!"

Marvin jumped up. "Steady on!" he said, "Don't take this efficiency expert business too literally; you're only pretending you know."

Henry sighed, "Look Marvin, you have sunk into departmental apathy. None of you are being objective. You have no real purpose. That's why you are getting on each other's nerves."

Marvin sat down. "What do you suggest?" he asked.

Henry thought for a moment. "Why don't we organise a 'Bonding Session' for the staff? We could involve them in setting out the cemetery and sleeping under the stars, then finish off with a concert in the rehearsal hall. It's a chance to see everyone in a new light and involve them in the project. We certainly need some extra hands. Can you sell it to the Mayor?"

Marvin rubbed his chin thoughtfully and Henry wondered briefly whether there was someone in a cubicle who should be doing it for him.

Chapter 44

That weekend the hillside was covered with people. Some clustered together nervously feeling threatened by the fresh air and space. There was a smattering of bright yellow rubber washing- up gloves belonging to the serious weekend weed-worriers.

Wellington boots shone with trendy designs and bright colours. Percy drew crowds as people admired his retro versions and one chap had his photo taken with him thinking he was a scarecrow!

Cuthbert had to admit that the influx of hands was useful even if there didn't seem to be a lot of brains to power them. Shovels became 'air guitars' and wheelbarrows were a complete mystery to the majority of them. All the coffins had been stored, except for the ones Silas took. The main job was to mark out the new plots, cut the grass and leave the rest for the digger.

Margery was the temporary nurse, it was her job to wait for the blisters and say, "There-there," in a sympathetic manner.

Marvin had mustered his troops, and now he sidled up to Henry. He seemed nervous, "Er, is this some kind of trick? Is Ronald going to sneak up behind them, use a garrotte and drop them into the holes?"

Henry looked at him calmly, "No."

Marvin persisted, "Drop lots of them in one hole then?"

Henry repeated, "No."

Marvin became distraught, "Please tell me there is a hole for Doreeen!" he wailed.

Henry squeezed his arm, "Not in front of the troops Marvin, all will be revealed."

Marvin wandered amongst his staff oblivious to the friendly banter. *I must have missed that course*, he thought.

The Captain came down to where Henry was standing.

Henry had been hearing loud 'yelps' for some time now and he asked the Captain what was going on.

The Captain smiled, "Some fool gave Percy a retractable thirty foot tape measure. He keeps pulling it out to its full extent, marching off, then forgetting about it and letting go! The yelp is the unfortunate on the other end."

Henry shook his head, "Has he done much damage?"

The Captain said, "Let's put it this way, if I had a nickel for every knuckle, I wouldn't be standing here!"

Cuthbert and Marvin were arguing about something and approaching rapidly when the Captain glanced downhill. "What's all that dust in the Valley?

There seemed to be some sort of wagon train stuck at the bridge and a man was making his way up towards them. Some of the dust was coming from the dry track, but quite a bit was coming from the man approaching. "Anyone know him?" asked Henry, aware that Silas may not give up easily.

Marvin shaded his eyes and gasped, "It is Mister Mason, the Master Mason and his son."

Cuthbert said, "Speaking of sun, shouldn't you start wearing a hat? There is only one of them!"

The man came gasping up to them with sweat lines running through the dust on his face. Recovering his breath, Mister Mason announced, "One memorial wall, all complete and delivered, as promised." He stood before them quivering with pride.

Marvin gaped, gasped and spluttered, "Finished, done, delivered... but... but! The last one took thirty years didn't it?"

Mister Mason beamed with pride. "Oh yes, but this is the Local Authority, so I sent it to be laser etched at great expense and here it is. You did say it was a rush job!"

Marvin was helped into a sitting position and left, while Henry organised teams to fetch the marble slabs up to the site.

The office workers were stunned. This sounded awfully like manual work and rubber gloves were expensive! Henry promised them a surprise and told them that each person could pick which team carried which slab.

They set off downhill muttering at this strange instruction.It was obvious some time later that the teams understood. Each slab was being carried reverently by the people named upon it.

Marvin was astonished as each team stopped and shook his hand before moving on. *Was this popularity?*

Henry winked at the others and whispered, "Two hundred down, one to go, keep an eye out for Doreeen!"

The whole site was lit by sudden flashes as people were photographed by their names, and Marvin was in great demand to share the poses. He was giddy from the admiration! He walked on air between his teams and shared drinks and sandwiches with them. He was suddenly Nelson, adored by his crew.

Henry walked over to Marvin some time later, and asked, "Right, who is on the hit-list then. How many holes do we need?"

Marvin blushed and replied bashfully, "You know, they're not a bad bunch at all. I have been invited to four barbecues and a christening. I rather think that the hit-list was a bit hasty."

Henry smiled and patted Marvin on the shoulder, which suddenly tensed as Henry asked, "Is that Doreeen?"

Henry sent Marvin back to his staff as they were spreading a gingham tablecloth and clearing a space for him and, signalling to the Captain to accompany him, they intercepted the woman.

Doreen was out of breath, so Henry managed quite a speech before she recovered. He introduced himself and the Captain and revealed that he was the one who had phoned and invited her to join them. He explained that, "It was only fair that she should see the way her husband was respected by his staff and share the kudos of this new project."

Doreen glared at Henry. Her hair was tied up in a severe bun and she peered through gun-slit spectacles. "What project? That silly little man has never achieved anything in his life. The tweed jacket's buttons strained against the ample bosom as she squared up to the two men.

"Who the devil are you?" she snapped at the Captain.

Henry patiently repeated his introduction and Doreen scoffed, "Military eh! No time for them. Father was military. How many men did *you* send to the mortuary?"

The Captain recoiled, "How on earth did you hear about that?"

She waved him to silence. "Where is that loser of mine?" she demanded.

Henry pointed, "He is over there, having a picnic with friends from the office." He began to walk forwards and she reluctantly followed him.

"Friends, him, from the office, have you got the right man?" She peered ahead just as Marvin stood and shaking hands all round, moved on to another group. She watched as Marvin acknowledged salutes, handshakes and mock bowing from everyone there.

As Doreen approached her husband, she began to notice that some of his admirers were rather young. Some of them were rather pretty too! She began to rapidly calculate his accumulated pension and perks and her survival instincts took over.

Henry paused politely as Doreen took her jacket off to reveal a white silk blouse straining at the leash. She then removed a device similar to a mole trap and her hair cascaded down onto her shoulders. The skirt was hitched up and Doreen managed to walk as if on stiletto heels. "Darling!" she cried as she flung her arms around Marvin's neck.

Marvin stood back and spluttered, "D... D ... Doreeeeen?"

"Of course darling, who else would come all this way to admire her husband?" she oozed. Taking him by the arm and leading him away from the girl who worked the photocopier.

Henry turned to the Captain. "Well," he began. "I think Marvin is starting with a clean slate." Then seeing his friend's downcast expression, he asked, "How many men *did* you send to the morgue?"

"Actually, it was about twelve," he replied uncomfortably. "It was Spiffy's promotion bash and I piled them all into the back of an ambulance at the end of the night, but I forgot to give the driver the address of the hotel, so they spent the weekend lying in refrigerated drawers down at the morgue. Spiffy still has the tag they tied to his toe!"

Henry smiled at his friend and they sat down at one of the picnics.

Chapter 45

Silas was fuming. His first delivery had arrived, but it would only cover his outlay. He wouldn't be in profit until the second load. He seemed to have lost Jasper and the Valley Mafia, and Cuthbert was making a great job of the cemetery.

His contact at the Local Authority, Marvin seemed to be in love, he never returned his calls. He had a coffin of nuclear waste at his rented house wreathed in a malevolent silence. This was the only one to survive the slide down the tunnels. The rest had been scrapped. Most of them had been empty. The only one with anything in it was full of receipts and burial records.

How Cuthbert had survived in the modern world was beyond him. The problem was to get the coffin in amongst the rest so that it could disappear and give him time to plan a new strategy. Donner und Blitzen could not get through the tunnels and he certainly couldn't push it back there alone. How to get a body buried in a cemetery. Surely it couldn't be that hard?

The cemetery was all laid out. All the paths were laid and the plots were marked out in white tape. Green lengths of fake grass covered the graves and all that was left to do was replace the coffins. Cuthbert, Percy, Henry, Ronald, and the Captain, would handle that next week. Tonight, Marvin's staff would be treated to a concert.

Silas had inspiration. He would offer Cuthbert the coffin full of paperwork as a peace offering and then switch the coffins, so that they buried it for him! He donned his funeral finery and began to prepare.

Percy was alone at the cemetery. Everyone else was taking it in turns to arm-wrestle Cuthbert's water pump in an attempt to spruce themselves up. Percy was preparing to add the finishing touch, but he had mislaid the flag. Hearing the sound of hooves on the new path, Percy went over to greet Silas.

"Wonderful job, Percy," said Silas through gritted teeth. "Where can I find Cuthbert?"

Percy explained that there was only him. The rest had gone to get ready for the evening.

Silas saw an opportunity. "Cuthbert agreed to have two of the coffins back. Sentimental value apparently." He opened the back of the carriage and Percy saw one coffin behind the glass top half and another one under the floor. Silas lifted the end of the lid and Percy glimpsed the piles of burial records Cuthbert had been searching for. "I think we should disappear these for him don't you?" purred Silas.

Percy agreed, especially if he could sneak some of them out to torment Cuthbert with at a later date.

"I'll give you a hand," said Percy's new friend.

Percy waved into the blackness as the horse-drawn hearse disappeared into the night and he returned to the coffins ready to stuff incriminating evidence down his wellies.

The first lid was solid, but a calculated blow from Percy's spade soon ended its reluctance and an eerie glow emanated from the hole.

"Ooh!" said Percy. Filling the spaces around the top of his wellies from the contents of the less dramatic second coffin, Percy set off for the rehearsal, discovering a new talent on the way.

Hands in pockets = darkness, hands out of pockets = green light showing him the way. All the way back, he skipped along happily chanting, "Now you see me, now you don't..."

Chapter 46

The rehearsal room was full. Most of the orchestra still looked like survivors from 'the battle for the lost chord', but they were keen to begin. The piano from the 'snug' at the Mandrake Arms was wheeled in; its little brass castors squealing in protest.

Il Maestro insisted upon playing wearing a blindfold. Some thought he was just showing off, but it was to stop him from seeing the state of this piano and crying his eyes out.

Samantha was becoming agitated. The Captain had kindly stepped up to join the violin section and Ronald was trying to appear 'macho' whilst holding up a triangle.

Henry surprised everyone by demonstrating a flare for the saxophone and Percy insisted upon standing in front of Samantha; whichever way she turned.

Cuthbert had been press-ganged into page turning for Il Maestro, and Percy was *still* in front of Samantha; whichever way she turned. Percy on top of the logistics of assembling a broken orchestra with a shattered pianist was just too much.

"What do you want?" she shrieked at him, voice cutting through even the strangled jangling sounds of tuning.

Percy looked down shamefaced. He scuffed the soles of his wellies on the floor and apologised for all his past demeanours. He then asked, "Is it not written that *If Mozart had taken to the shoe-making trade, his music may have been cobblers?*"

Samantha stared.

Percy grinned.

Samantha still stared as her humourless brain tried to connect her hero with shoe repairs, and by the time Samantha had regained her poise Percy was ensconced behind the timpani and the conductor was tapping for attention.

Samantha walked to her doom in a trance-like state.

The audience was enthralled. The 1812 overture saw Percy power the orchestra through the cannon fire of Austerlitz and replicate the artillery barrages of modern warfare.

The orchestra was driven.

Henry switched to a trumpet to sound the retreat and the audience was on its feet for the finale.

Cameras flashed and Percy seemed to be the main focus of attention. The odd thing was; the camera flashes seemed to be sending his hands green! The cries of 'Encore 'could not be ignored.

Cuthbert flicked the pages rather hard in his excitement and slapped Il Maestro around the ear.

The blindfolded pianist swung around losing his sense of quite where the piano was and his fingers were air-borne again.

Cuthbert tried to spin him back and caught a lever on the side of the piano. Jangling rag-time jazz filled the hall!

Henry reached for the saxophone and wailed to the stars in accompaniment.

Percy beat out a thumping heartbeat and the double bass added the foot tapping pulse.

Il Maestro had moved to the end of his stool and jumped every time the mechanical handle completed a revolution and struck him.

During a break in one of the riffs, Henry shouted to Cuthbert, "Look at Percy's hands. Has he been at the glow sticks again?"

Marvin glided home on a cloud of adoration, linked arm in arm with a transformed Doreen and with the Mayor's praises ringing in his ears, a formal ceremony would take place to unveil the monument to the fallen heroes of the Local Authority and the grand re-opening of the cemetery.

There was the odd glitch still to iron out, like how to explain the cost of the slabs of laser-etched Padua marble and gold-leaf work to the general public.

Marvin assumed that there would be another 'Valleys in Bloom' flower contest this year, where all the hanging baskets were donated and the costs of the memorial could disappear as 'paying for the prizes for that wonderful display in the *other* valley.'

Around Cuthbert's table, there was a silence as they all sat in the dark and watched Percy glow.

Chapter 47

The next morning was a typical Valley day, the sky was clear. In fact, it was the only thing in the Valley which was ever clear, everything else was utter confusion.

The cooking range seemed to be sulking and huffily refused to open any of its doors, and the kettle had no intention of whistling.

Cuthbert wandered outside and admired his kingdom. His gaze stopped at the sight of a building with a double roof, but he soon connected this with the fact that one of his outbuildings had no roof at all. He must ask Percy about that.

Percy shambled downstairs and eyed the kitchen range; it rumbled and let out a puff of smoke and a dribble of ash as they prepared to out-stare each other.

Cuthbert watched the sleek black shape of a hearse approaching rapidly. The hearse fish-tailed as it negotiated a bend. It would have shaken itself to bits before Aunt Liza had repaired and flattened all the roads and paths. The owner of the crematorium shook his fist at Cuthbert as he screeched to a halt in a cloud of smoke from burning tyres. The beautifully maintained chrome radiator was slightly marred by a piece of mouldy mangled timber projecting from it. This was almost certainly part of Cuthbert's gate.

The irate driver leapt out of the car. "Who did it, where is he, was it you, was it him?"

The raging driver found himself face to face with Cuthbert's first (and last) line of defence, *inscrutability.*

Cuthbert recognised the man as the owner of the 'Heavenly Way Internment complex,' but he didn't remember his face being quite as red as this. Deciding to be professional, Cuthbert gave the man the endearing smile he reserved for relatives of the recently deceased.

The man took a step back in alarm just as Percy stepped outside. "My angel, my angel!" cried the man, running forward with his arms outstretched.

Cuthbert's smile froze and Percy's eyes widened, but the man ran past them both and embraced a stone angel propped up against the wall.

Dragging the trumpet-playing visitation from heaven to the back of his hearse and sliding it safely inside, the man pointed at Cuthbert and Percy. His finger was long and pointed and it quivered to match the quaver in his voice as he ranted, "It was *you, It was you!* Don't think I don't know who put fireworks in Mr. Belshaw's pockets either. He blew the crematorium doors off yesterday! You haven't heard the last of this."

"I'm only just hearing the *first* of this," muttered Cuthbert risking a glance at Percy.

The hearse completed a 180 degree turn, rocking on its suspension as it did so, and thundered off down the drive narrowly missing the Captain and Henry.

Each of them had seen the heavenly wings and the raised trumpet through the glass as the hearse bounced past.

"Typical," said Henry, "An angel comes to earth and those two fossilise it."

"Maybe that's why they call them 'Stiffs'," suggested the Captain.

Cuthbert was ranting at Percy, "What did you want with a stone angel?"

"Saved me blowing my own trumpet," grinned Percy.

"Mr. Belshaw?" demanded Cuthbert.

"Ah," said Percy just as the Captain and Henry joined them. "He was the head of the gardener's federation and I was always giving him advice."

"Did he ask for any?" asked Henry.

Percy ignored him and sat on the stile shuffling to get comfortable. The other three looked at each other in horror; they hadn't even had a cup of tea yet.

"The trouble with these local federations and societies," began Percy, "Is that they get set in their ways, they only grow the same old flowers, discuss the same old fertilisers and agree with each other all the time. So, when I decided to reveal an old family secret, it didn't go down very well."

The crow sat behind them and watched as Percy glanced at everyone in turn, hoping for someone to make a mistake and ask, "What was that Percy?"

The silence stretched until it hummed like an elastic band. The crow would have raised an eyebrow, but all his feathers went the wrong way, so instead with a glint of mischief he supplied, "Caw?"

142

That was enough for Percy, "One of the greatest tragedies of the past was the failure of the rice crop in Ireland…"

"Don't you mean potatoes?" barked the Captain.

"That's right, it was a potato famine Percy," said Henry.

Cuthbert stayed silent, he'd been here before.

Percy sat on the stile swinging his little legs backwards and forwards and shaking his head from side to side.

Cuthbert thought that his friend looked like a garden gnome keeping time to the music, in which case it would make Percy a 'Metro-gnome'.

With a suspicious look at the smirk on Cuthbert's face, Percy ploughed on, "Common mistake chaps, but the truth is that the potatoes were only planted to make up for the failure of the rice crop, but because nobody had cleared the fields of rice properly, it caused the potato crop to fail as well."

"Caw?" said the crow, ducking down before pieces of dry-stone-wall began coming his way.

"People tried everything," said Percy shuffling again. "Some even sailed to America looking for suggestions, but there must have been a problem with immigration because they didn't come back."

The silence hummed again until Henry resignedly sighed, "Go on Percy."

"Well," he said, "They sent for my ancestor, Paddy Plumm, who had planted the original fields and he announced that the rice must have been planted upside down and he mobilised whole villages clearing out the old potatoes and then clearing every grain of rice before replanting them."

"Did it succeed?" cried his audience.

"W-e-e-l-l," said Percy hesitantly, "He was the hero of the county until the new seed arrived and it didn't look anything like the stuff they had just removed."

"What was it then?" asked three voices at once.

"Caw?" asked another.

Percy hesitated and looked around sheepishly, "Well, when Paddy was at the docks looking for supplies to plant the fields the first time, he spotted a ship from the Orient unloading. He went over and checked out the merchandise, there was a very delicate white paper laid out and Paddy admired it saying, "Nice paper.""

A man with a pigtail nodded enthusiastically, scrunched a piece up and popped it into his mouth saying, "Yes, rice-paper."

Paddy tried a piece and as it dissolved on his tongue, he spotted a pile of empty bags he would need to transport the rice he bought. Pointing to them, he said, "Nice bags."

The pigtail bobbed enthusiastically again as the trader confirmed, "Yes, rice-bags."

"So, of course, Paddy put two and two together and assumed that the rice-bags would dissolve the same way as the rice-paper did and he took a pile of them home with him where the other farmers chucked them into the furrows, covered them in soil and waited for them to grow."

"Which they didn't?" asked Henry with a sarcastic tone.

Percy sighed, "No, and neither did the potatoes they chucked in afterwards. To this day they call them Paddy Fields."

The four friends trooped dejectedly towards Cuthbert's kitchen. Even the crow thought that a cup of tea might just do the trick.

Chapter 48

The day of the opening ceremony was clear and sunny and the whole Local Authority was given a holiday with all its vital responsibilities handled by a single answer-phone.

The gravel paths were raked smooth, the grave areas were well-tended and had flowers on each and every one of them.

The newly dug plots were sensitively covered with sheets of artificial grass. Of course, Percy discovered this the hard way when he sat on one to eat his sandwiches and disappeared.

The effect of the monument was amazing, vertical slabs spaced slightly apart topped off with a long thin lintel giving a Stonehenge effect.

People were posing for photographs in front of the slabs bearing their names and the carnival atmosphere aided by the Valley Mafia seemed to have painted their hands green and joined in the fun, in fact when the sun shone directly on them, *they glowed.*

Cuthbert was trying to bask in the glory of the moment, but it was difficult with some of the comments directed at him, "Better than that dump you had up here Cuthbert." Or, "Now *this* is worth dying for now." And, "Did my Mum ever turn up Cuthbert?"

Percy was in conversation with one of the young female typists after he stood on her dress and she couldn't escape.

Out of desperation, she tried, "Were you bullied at school for being a redhead?"

Percy saw an opening for the sympathy vote and sighed, "Oh yes, when I was young other kids smeared me with whipped cream and chocolate and the put a cherry on my head," pausing for effect. "It was a hard life in the gateau," he added solemnly.

The girl gaped.

The Mayor insisted upon Avril reporting the opening on behalf of the Triple Echo and she was forced to trudge behind him ready to jot down any pearls of wisdom he was prepared to share with the world, so far her notebook was empty.

The Mayor himself was thrilled with the whole concept of commemorating those heroes of the Local Authority who had fallen to the pressures whilst he himself had stood firm, and of course, he had convinced himself that it had all been his idea.

Narrowing his eyes and peering up at the top left hand corner of the first slab, he spotted his name, just where that chap, 'what's-is-name,' had said it would be. But, as he peered higher, he thought he saw more writing on the lintel itself. *Jolly good, that must be the council's motto in Latin, can't read it from here though.*

"Anyone got a stepladder?" he called out to the milling minions.

Percy was trying to figure out where the girl had disappeared to and why he had a piece of floral material stuck to the bottom of his welly, when he realised that he had company, if you could call being surrounded by the Valley Mafia, *company* that is.

The crow had been circling above waiting for the innocent girl to move away from Percy, and when she made her escape he lined up his beak to the target and began his bomb-run. Seeing the Valley Mafia encircle his target caused him to tighten his tail feathers and abort the mission, 'Sorry chaps,' he muttered, 'If this lot have their catapults, the flak would be horrendous, returning to base.'

Jasper detached himself from the circle and stood before Percy. "Nice day, Percy," said the leader of the Valley Mafia.

"Sure is," replied Percy, narrowing his eyes gunfighter style.

"I notice that your hands are green there Percy," Jasper hissed.

"Gardener… green fingers," hissed Percy in return.

"*We're* not gardeners," accused Jasper.

The whole circle of Valley Mafia held up their hands, palms outwards, and they all glowed green.

"You been opening boxes, Percy?" asked Jasper.

Percy hesitated.

"Get him lads," said Jasper.

Marvin felt the fingers of dread clasp his heart as he saw the stepladder being carried forward, he had no reason to fear anything, but when life is suddenly this good there is usually a trick lined up somewhere.

He looked around desperately for the stone-mason and grabbed him by the arm, instantly regretting it as he choked on the dust caused by the sudden contact.

146

"What is that engraved along the top?" croaked Marvin.

The stonemason beamed proudly, "It's exactly what you gave me on the original notes Mr. Middlewick. Scrupulous in my file keeping, I am," and he began to rummage through many and varied pockets causing more dust to envelop the pair of them.

The stonemason had a calming effect on Marvin, probably because he styled himself *Mister Mason, Master Mason & Son*. Marvin liked things in triplicate.

"Aaaah!" cried the stonemason, waving a sheet of paper to dislodge even more dust into the atmosphere, "Here it is."

Marvin lost control and snatched the paper, his heart constricted as he read a title across the top *Know thine enemies*, it read, *Smite them on my road to power.*

"Why?" he spluttered, waving the paper. "What made you think?" he spluttered even more.

Mister Mason scratched his head, dislodging a stream of dust from a job that even he could not remember. "But it was written right across the top, that why I made a lintel to get it all on."

Marvin looked around wildly, the Mayor was starting to climb, a crowd was gathering and the Valley Mafia was disappearing down a hole one by one.

"Come on," demanded Marvin dragging the stonemason along. If he was going down, at least he would have an accomplice.

Percy sat in the gloom of an underground crypt; members of the mafia were still dropping into the hole and forming a circle around him. When everyone was in place, they raised their hands to illuminate the space with a green glow. Percy's hands stayed in his lap.

Jasper's voice was soft with menace, "We know you are in league with Silas, how much is he paying you Percy?"

Percy glanced around quickly looking for the exit, but it wasn't easy to judge distances when bathed in a radioactive glow.

"*How Much?*" snapped Jasper, seeing his profits threatened.

Percy made an attempt at levity, "As in, how much wood would a wood chuck, chuck, if a woodchuck could chuck wood?"

The silence gave Percy an idea of how badly he had failed, especially when a voice hissed, "More like, how much muck could the Mafia chuck, if the Mafia buried a chump?"

Percy gulped.

The Mayor was at the top of the stepladder now and fumbling for his glasses.

The crowd waited expectantly and Marvin urged his brain into a stampede of inspiration; if the cavalry were coming over the hill, it looked as if they had chosen the wrong one.

The Mayor's lips moved silently as his eyes moved along the carved letters. "If this is the Local Authority's motto, shouldn't it be in Latin?" he asked.

Marvin gulped and replied, "Well Mr. Mayor, we tried for a Latin motto for the cemetery itself, but we had some trouble with it. 'Always speak well of the dead' was tricky, and 'In memory of the dead' was tricky too, because of the confusion of Cuthbert's cemetery, people often popped back to photograph their own gravestones, so you never knew who you were speaking well of."

The crowd was silent as the Mayor climbed down and waited for the ladder to be moved so that he could read the rest.

Marvin's neck reddened as he sensed 'Doreeen's' gaze upon him.

Percy sighed dramatically, "Alright lads, you've started to show the first signs of living in the Valley, but your superpowers aren't as well developed as mine so let's stop messing about shall we?"

"What superpowers?"

"Look out boys, it's Turnip-Man!" cried another.

Percy waited for the hysterics to die down before he reignited them by jamming his glowing green hands deep inside his wellies.

"He's disappeared!" shouted someone.

"He's invisible!" shouted someone else.

Panic stricken green hands flapped in all directions as the Mafia suddenly found itself in the dark with an unseen entity, they broke with tradition and ran.

Marvin was temporarily distracted by the sight of the Valley Mafia appearing out of a hole and fleeing in all directions while Percy climbed out after them, dusted himself down and wandered over to see what all the fuss was about.

Cuthbert meanwhile had been attracted to a glowing mound just behind the memorial and he was rummaging through an old coffin which had been sloppily covered in fake grass sheeting. He knew it was one of his because there were several names inscribed in the lid and then crossed out again. As he squeezed past another coffin where the glow was coming from, it seemed to sink further into the ground and even seemed to give out a gentle vibration.

The Mayor looked down from the top of the ladder and recited the wording of the lintel, "Know thine enemies – smite them on my road to power," he read. "This isn't a memorial," he said, "It's a hit-list."

The crowd gave out a collective gasp and everyone turned to stare at Marvin. Unfortunately, this included the man who was steadying the ladder and the Mayor was forced into an undignified sliding descent.

Marvin knew that this was the moment to turn on the charm, but he had absolutely no idea how to do it, so he began to back away even though this seemed to invite the crowd to advance.

"I can explain," he spluttered before hearing those dreaded words...

"Well go on then."

"Er, it's a directive... 'Know thine enemies... planning opponents... journalists... people who want to know where their taxes went."

Marvin was sweating and still backing off, but the crowd had slowed down and many heads were nodding in agreement until the Mayor demanded, "And what about 'Smite them on MY road to power, do you have ambitions Marvin?"

Marvin heard a snort which could only have come from Doreeen, and he quickly pulled Mister Mason to his side,

"That's his fault, it should read THY road to power, his ears are full of dust." ... "Aren't they?" he whispered to the stonemason.

"Heh?" asked Mister Mason on cue.

Marvin sensed his moment. He squared his shoulders and forced his way through the crowd until his back was to the monument and the whole of the Local Authority staff and most of the Valley folk were forced to look up at him in the fading light.

He raised his arms for silence. "This motto should inspire all Local Authority workers in the quest," he began.

"Quest?" shouted Percy. "Is there an Easter egg hunt?"

149

Marvin ignored him and raised his arms even higher, so that the crowd would see him in the dusk, "The quest for perfection, the need to make the public conform to our great standards and traditions, they must stop counting our paperclips."

"That's my job," whispered someone proudly. Marvin continued and behind him, the monument began to glow!

"Ooo-err," said the crowd in unison as they stepped back a pace.

Marvin could see that he was inspiring them so his oratory rose to new heights. "We will NOT reveal our expenses and free doughnuts," he cried as the glowing monument silhouetted him in all his glory. Never in the fields of road-works and bridge-building, have so many people owed so much to so few; we will fight them on the playing fields of Eton and increase the council tax to pay for it all," he raged.

The monument was throbbing with colour and the glow was starting to light the sky. Cuthbert had appeared with arms full of his missing filing system, just as the Captain and Henry grabbed Marvin and they all headed downhill as quickly as possible.

At the bottom of the hill the crowd gaped upwards as if with a final flare, the monument sank into the hill and disappeared.

The crowd slowly meandered away into the night with various groups forming to chat and then splitting up again like a shoal of fish.

The Mayor kept pace with Marvin and whispered, "I'm not really sure what happened up there, but I think we should forget about it as long as you promise not to run for Mayor."

Marvin nodded silently and smiled, he could feel the weight of the Mayoral chain around his neck already.

Chapter 49

Percy was pulling random sheets of paper out of the pile Cuthbert was carrying, reading them and basically tossing them behind him. "Who was B. Read?" he asked.

"I can't remember," muttered Cuthbert trying to see over the pile. "Why?"

Percy peered at the paper in the gloom, saying, "Well, apparently you buried him with C. Heese, F. Lour and P. Ears.

"Either you like your bodies to keep each other company or you've just salvaged four years of shopping lists."

Cuthbert groaned and tried to make a mental note of where he had just thrown the pile of papers in the dark.

Percy skipped ahead in high spirits totally unaware of the trip-wire and all the tight vibrating catapult elastics aimed at him from the darkness ahead.

Henry, Marjorie, and the Captain, flanked the Mayor as soon as he was alone.

"Quite a display that," said the Captain.

"Expensive too, I would have thought," said Henry.

"Another 'Valley in Bloom' contest this year then?" suggested Marjorie.

"I expect so," sighed the Mayor.

"Same rules as last year then, we win if the Mafia stays in their own Valley?"

"That would be nice," said a dejected Mayor.

"Jolly good," said the Captain.

~ The End ~

About the Author

Patrick Barrett is a sixty year old ex-miner from Mansfield in Nottinghamshire. He is married to Paula and between them, they have several children. 'Shakespeare's Cuthbert' was his first book, though he has been writing comedy for several years.

His aims as a writer are 'to be successful and make people laugh by providing them with an escape from the harshness of real life'.

His other abiding interest is in antiques.